Tales From Here There and Everywhere

50 Short Stories
by
Don Conway

Copyright © 2016 Don Conway

ISBN: 978-0-692-76739-9

PublishNation LLC
www.publishnation.net

For my son Russell

Also by this author

HUMAN RESPONSE TO TALL BUILDINGS, D.Conway Ed.
Dowden, Hutchinson and Ross, Inc. 1977

ACKNOWLEDGEMENTS

Critique, feedback and much love from the Royal Palm Beach Writers Group made this project possible.

Russell Conway and Kathi Conway were my "Go for It" team. Wendy Jacobs edited my errors and omissions with grace and Oksana Lamankina produced the drawings you see here with professionalism and dedication.

CONTENTS

Prologue

I like riding on trains. Don't you? Long train rides are the best. They give you the opportunity to glimpse many cities and towns, and they are all different; each one has its shape, form, and character. Some places may look familiar to you, and some will be like nothing you have ever seen before. That's what makes a train ride such an adventure — if you open your mind to it.

Think of the stories in this book as a train ride. I will be your conductor. As we take this fantastic train ride together, I will try to take you to some places that are familiar and some that are like nothing you have ever seen before. What I can promise you is that each story will have its own shape, form and character.

The stories (towns) that I am going to take you to are the distilled memories and experiences of my life which, like the best of train rides, has been a long one. So climb aboard and let's get this adventure started.

Don Conway
Florida, 2016

1

CLIP-CLOP

Clip-Clop. Clip-Clop.

This is going to be tough, sergeant CB thought to herself. *Two tours in Afghanistan had been hard, but this might be harder. I guess I knew that when I volunteered for this duty. Has it only been nine weeks since I started training? So much to learn . . . caring for the horses, polishing the bridles and saddles, how to sit at attention in the saddle, the protocols for each type of funeral.*

Clip-Clop. Clip-Clop.

Well, I'm here now, officially a member of the Caisson Platoon of the Old Guard, 3rd United States Infantry. Arlington is so beautiful on a fall day like this. The sun is warm, and the trees have turned colors. And quiet. The horse's hoof beats are almost the only sound.

Clip-Clop. Clip-Clop

I'm really grateful to the Sergeant Major for stopping by the stables this morning. He knows this is my first funeral. "Not to worry CB," he said. "Just remember you're a Sergeant in the Old Guard. You know how important this ceremony is to the family. It means they can finally bring closure to this difficult time. Your job is to maintain the dignity of the funeral. That's how we show the family that we are sharing their loss." That was really helpful.

Clip-Clop. Clip-Clop

I have a good mount this morning. They call her Mom. She's a gentle, steady horse. I wonder how many funerals like this she has been part of? She makes me think of my Mom, gentle and steady, always there. Even when I decided to re-up in the Army.

Clip-Clop. Clip-Clop.

I didn't mean to, but I got a glimpse of the family while the casket was being placed on the caisson. Two older couples. Parents I suppose. A young woman —wife? And a small boy about six or seven. I wonder if he really understands what is happening here. Perhaps one day he will. They are following along quietly behind the caisson now.

Clip-Clop. Clip-Clop.

Almost at the grave site. There's the Casket Team waiting for us. Be sure to hold the horses steady while they lift the casket off the caisson. There, that's done. Wait a bit while the team and the family walk to the grave site.

They're gone now. Time for us to leave.

Yes, she thought, *this is a privilege and I can do it. But why must there be so many funerals. . . .*

Clip-Clop. Clip-Clop.

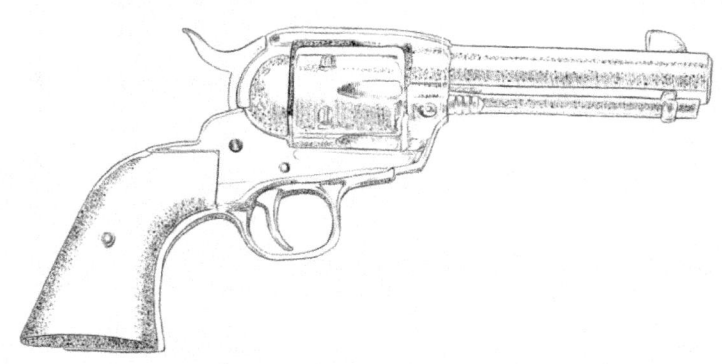

2

THE LUCK OF THE IRISH

The gunshot broke the silence of the almost-empty warehouse. "Put that thing away." Paulie the Iceman said.

"I just wanted to be sure it was working." Loco replied.

"Of course it works. It's a gun you dummy."

"You shouldn't oughta talk to me like that."

"But I told you, this is a simple, safe job. I don't even know why you brought that thing with you."

"You told me I'm supposed to protect you."

"Yeah, yeah. I know that's what I said, But I also told you there won't be anyone here but some old man of a watchman. All you have to do is sit on him while I crack this safe, which is about a hundred years old. A piece of cake— ten, maybe fifteen minutes, tops."

"Well that's the problem," Loco said. "I can't just sit on him."

"Waddya mean, you can't sit on him? You was a professional wrestler. You got muscles coming outta your ears. You telling me you can't handle an old man?"

"The old man is not the problem. Judge Wilson is the problem. He says I am a hardened criminal and a two-time loser, and if he sees me in his courtroom again, he is sending me up the river for life. So there cannot be no witnesses to this here simple safe job."

"What! You telling me you are going to whack this old guy?"

"Only if I have to."

"Why didn't you tell me this before I hired you?"

"You didn't ask."

"Okay, okay, but we're here now. So let's see if we can get this over with before the old man comes around."

Both men crept to the corner office where the safe was located. Paulie the Iceman put on his stethoscope and proceeded to work on the safe. About five minutes into the operation, Loco poked him in the shoulder and whispered in his ear "He's coming."

"For God's sake don't put no holes in him. Bring him in here and let's see what develops."

Three minutes later, Loco came back into the office dragging an elderly watchman in a ragged uniform and wearing a coat and hat. The watchman was clearly terrified. Loco literally tossed the old man into a chair.

"Okay," Paulie said. "Don't do nothing 'til I finish wid this here safe. Just watch him." Paulie returned to his work and ten minutes later he swung open the safe door. He tossed aside papers and file folders until he uncovered a small box and opened it.

"Very nice, very nice," the Iceman said. "Off hand I would say twenty to thirty grand of lovely jewels. Your cut is maybe six or seven grand," he said to Loco.

"Okay, so now I whack the old man and we go, right?"

"Wait a minute. Let me think," Paulie admonished.

He started pacing the floor trying to think of the next move. While he was pacing, Loco moved in on the terrified old man cowering in the chair. He looked him over, much like a hungry fox appraising a chicken. When his glance came to the name tag pinned to the old man's coat he stopped, riveted by what he saw written on it

"Your name is O'Malley?" Loco asked

"Yes, Patrick O'Malley."

"Do you know Detective O'Malley of the 73rd Police Station?"

"Do you mean Danny O'Malley?"

"Yeah, that's the one."

"Yes, he's my son."

"You're Danny O'Malley's old man?"

"Yes."

"Detective O'Malley is a good guy. He testified on my behalf at my last trial. Because of his testimony the judge cut my time up the river to three years instead of ten. I owe your son Danny a big favor."

"That's it!" exclaimed Pauliet the Iceman. "You owe the old man's son a big favor so we don't have to whack him." He turned to the old man. "Listen," he said, "this guy is facing life in prison if you finger him for this robbery. So he is about to shoot you through with many holes, which is very bad for your health. So here's the deal. Loco here, is going to bop you on the head so you can say we took you by surprise and you never saw a thing. To sweeten the deal I am even going to give you two or three of these pretty stones. And you can be sure that if you ever say anything to the cops, even to your son, we will come back and finish you off. So waddya say?"

"Well, I don't want to die. So okay, I'll go along with you."

No sooner said than done. Loco bopped O'Malley and the two thieves left the warehouse.

About an hour later when Irving Bauman came to, he thought to himself *That was close! Lucky for me that when I spilled the coffee on myself Pat O'Malley had left his jacket and name tag in the locker room.*

3

THERE'S NO PLACE LIKE HOME

I am sure you all know about Dorothy and her adventures in the Merry Old Land of Oz, and how she truly came to believe that "there's no place like home." What you may not know is that after her adventures in Oz, Dorothy continued to live on the farm, even after her Auntie Em and Uncle Henry had passed away, and their three farmhands moved on to other jobs. As she grew older, Dorothy learned to make apple pies and peach preserves.. Her peach preserves always won a blue ribbon at the county fair. And every day the bluebird of happiness would fly into the farmyard and sing to her. She truly believed that there was no place like home.

Eventually, Dorothy got married and had a little girl of her own, whom she named "Liza" (Liza with a Z). Dorothy tried her best to teach Liza the joys of "there's no place like home." She even tried to teach her daughter how to make apple pies and to preserve peaches, But Liza would have none of it. She grew up to be a contrary child with a wanderlust nature. When she entered her twenties, Liza decided she had enough of farm life and apple pies, and she set out to see the world.

One of the first places she went was to New York, New York, where she became a nightclub singer. New York, New York, was fine for her for awhile, but eventually she decided to see if she could find her own bluebird of happiness in England. She moved into four sordid rooms in Chelsea with her friend named Elsie.

Elsie turned out to be a Naughty Lady who led a very fast life, which brought about her death at a young age. "You see," cried Liza, "when I go, I'm going like Elsie."

She moved to Berlin in 1933 just as the Nazi Party was coming to power. While working in a Berlin nightclub, called "Cabaret," Liza met a young Englishman with whom she had a brief affair.

She became pregnant but decided that having a baby would end her singing career, so she gave the baby up for adoption. This drove her into a deep depression, which lasted for months and caused her to lose her singing job at Cabaret.

Forlorn, out of work, and stranded in a foreign country, Liza suddenly realized the truth of Dorothy's teaching that, "there's no place like home." So she sold all her belongings and bought a ticket for home. Once back in Kansas and on the farm, Liza learned to bake apple pies and preserve peaches and to listen to the bluebird of happiness as it sang in the farmyard every day. She truly came to believe that she must be living somewhere over the rainbow, and she lived happily ever after.

4

VIVA ESPAÑA

Madrid, Heart of Spain

Madrid, heart of Spain
Throbbing with the beats of fever.
If yesterday her blood was boiling
Today it boils with more heat.
She will never be able to sleep,
Because if Madrid falls asleep,
She will wish to wakeup one day
And dawn will not come to meet her.
Don't forget, Madrid, the war.
Never forget that in front
The eyes of the enemy
Are throwing at you looks of death.

-Rafael Alberti

By January 1937, the Nationalist forces of Spain's Francisco Franco were on the western side of the river Manzanares that ran from north to south and divided the city of Madrid almost in half. On the eastern side of the river, Republican militias were fighting from trenches that had been dug by the women and children of Madrid in preparation for the siege. Composed of socialist, Communists, various trade unions, and several international brigades, the militias were poorly armed and scarcely trained. Their Russian advisers were of some help, but Franco's Army of Africa with its Moroccan troops and divisions of the Spanish Foreign Legion had the advantage of German and Italian modern arms and professional officers.

Still, the militia troops had fought the Nationalists to a standstill...for the moment.

One advantage the militias had were their *dinamiteros*, of the miner's union. These were tough miners who were experts in tunneling and the use of dynamite. Their leader, by virtue of experience and aggressiveness, was a thirty-one-year-old named Rafael Escobedo. Since the start of the Madrid siege in October 1936, Rafael and his band of miners had dug several tunnels under strongholds of the Nationalist's troops and then blown them up killing many of Franco's troops and mortally wounding the morale of the Nationalist army. It was impossible to predict when or where the ground would suddenly erupt beneath your feet dealing death and destruction all around.

General Franco raged at his inability to stop the carnage of the *dinamiteros* and had placed a reward of twenty thousand pesos on the head of Rafael Escobedo to be captured dead or alive.

Rafael and his band of forty or fifty miners were billeted safely behind the front lines at the North Train Station. Working in day and night shifts, they ventured from the station to the latest tunnels. Between shifts, there was the nearby *taberna*, newly named Los Compañeros de Armás, where wine, spirits, and some food were available. A fortyish widow named Amália Rodriguez owned and ran the taberna with an iron will and a stern look for any of the miners who got out of hand. Her only employee and all-around handyman was an elderly Madrid native, who went by the single name of Horatio.

Living through the pressures of war often leads to the distortion of normal relationships. That was the case with

Rafael and the widow Rodriguez. The ever-present fear of death, the struggle of day-to-day survival, and the longing for companionship with someone to share these threats had led to their liaison...at least that was how Rafael explained it to himself. The widow had other motives in mind.

Amalia was a staunch Nationalist. She considered the execution of her husband at the hands of militia troops in 1935 a symbol of what the socialist and Communist forces among the Republicans would do to all Spaniards who showed any allegiance to the legitimate hereditary monarchy and its allies in the Catholic Church. She had vowed to have her revenge against the militias, and Rafael was the perfect target. The instrument of her revenge would be her brother, a sergeant in Franco's army now sitting just across the river.

The widow's plan was simple. Every evening as Rafael left to lead his miners to the tunnels he would say, "If I die tonight, the last memory I want to have is of your face. Stand in the road and let me look at you as I leave." That would be the opportune moment for Amalia's brother to kill him. All that was needed was a message to her brother telling him which day, and at what time, the killing should occur. Horatio, who could neither read nor write, could easily make his way across the Los Franceses Bridge to the other side of the river and deliver a letter to her brother.

The letter was written, and Amalia gave him explicit instructions on how to hide the letter and where to find her brother.

Though Horatio was an old man, he was not a fool. He knew where Amália's sympathies lay, and his instincts told him the letter was some form of treachery against the Republican forces. He took the letter to Rafael.

What a fool I was. Blinded by love Rafael thought.

"Don't worry, old man," he said to Horatio. "I know what needs to be done. Go ahead and follow your instructtions exactly. Deliver this letter and then leave everything to me."

Nine o'clock on a cold February night was the time set for the assassination. As Rafael was getting ready to leave for the tunnels he said, "If I die tonight, the last memory I want to have is of your face. Stand in the road and let me look at you as I leave. But wait, it is cold outside. Here, put my coat around your shoulders and my hat on your head. I will not need them tonight, and if you are warm, you can stand in the road a bit longer as I leave."

A single rifle shot rang out. Amália was dead before her body hit the ground.

"Viva España," Rafael murmured to himself as he walked away.

5

THE LETTER

A man named Bob walked into a neighborhood tavern in the Bronx and was greeted by friends.

"Hey Bob, back so soon? We didn't expect you for a few more days."

"It turns out the folks were okay after all. That long drive up to Boston was all for nothing. Still, you have to look out for your parents if you can," Bob replied.

Most of the friends nodded and murmured in agreement.

"But listen, guys," Bob said. "Something happened today on the trip back that I want to tell you about. And I need your advice."

"You know we'll help if we can," they answered.

Bob reached into his pocket and took out a small envelope. "On the way back I stopped at one of those service plazas on the New York State Thruway. I got a cup of coffee and went to sit in a booth. On the bench was this letter. It wasn't sealed, so to pass the time with my coffee, I opened it and read it. Maybe I shouldn't have. Let me read the letter to you and then maybe you can tell me what I should do with it."

First Bob read the envelope. "It's addressed to Mrs. Grace Ferguson, 936 Elm Street, Summerville, Iowa." He removed the letter from the envelope. "It's dated yesterday," Bob said, as he started to read.

My Dearest Grace,

Greetings from Hartford, Connecticut, the insurance capital of the United States. So far the convention is going great. Two days ago I attended a swell workshop on "How to Read Your

Annuity tables." There were plenty of handouts, and I think they are going to help me a lot when I get back to Summerville. Last night was the Winners' Banquet, and I was seated at a table with Mr Big himself... I actually had dinner with John Eberhard, 2016 Insurance Man of the Year.

So you can see, Grace, this trip away from you will be worth it in the end — that is, if we can get over one small problem. I don't know of any easy way to tell you this, so I'll just come out and say it. I've been turned into a Vampire!

Guess I better start at the beginning. After the banquet I was so keyed up I just knew I wouldn't be able to fall asleep, so I went to the hotel bar for a nightcap. And that's where I met her. Now, before you get upset, Grace, let me tell you that I have always been faithful to you. (I think you know that.) and at age fifty-five, bald and a bit overweight, we both know that I am not the philandering type.

Anyway, I guess it was the excitement of the banquet and a few drinks too many that led to a conversation with this woman. Well, Grace, she was awfully attractive, and somewhat sexy, so one thing led to another and before I knew it, we were up in her room. Honestly, Grace, I've never done anything like this before. Please believe me.

That woman lured me into her bed and then when there was no way to stop the proceedings she told me that she was a vampire. I knew right away that I ought to have run out of the room, but I was too much under her spell by that time. When she bit down on my neck, I thought it was just her idea of foreplay.

When I woke up this morning, she was gone. And now I have the strangest feelings', I find myself looking at people's throats, and I have constant hunger pains. Then I did the weirdest thing — but I couldn't help myself. I telephoned a

Funeral home in Summerville and ordered a casket. It will be delivered to you in a day or so.

Grace, I know this is going to be a difficult time for us. I have checked out of the convention hotel, and I am on my way home to you. I know, honey, that with you by my side, we can face this together.

I should be home by Friday.

Your loving husband,
Norman

Bob finished reading the letter, looked up at his friends and said, "So what do you think guys? Should I mail this letter to Mrs. Ferguson?"

6

FAMILY TRADITION

"Well, I don't know, Uncle Bill. Sometimes I get talked into the darnedest things..."

"Now, now, don't think of it that way, George. Remember, this is a family tradition. I've been doing this for twelve years, and if it weren't for that motorcycle accident, I'd still be doing it."

"Yeah, I know but it still seems sorta dangerous to me."

"No, no. Remember, this is show business. It's all an illusion. Look, I've explained the whole procedure to your mother, and she is satisfied it's safe. She even encouraged me to talk to you about doing it. Do you think I'd put my sister's only child in harm's way?"

"No, I don't think you'd intentionally do anything to harm me, but what about your brother, Uncle Fred? He-."

"What happened to your Uncle Fred was a freak accident, and everyone knows it. Fred had done it 315 times before his ... um ... tragic ending."

"Well O.K. If I agree to do it, what's the next step?"

"Atta boy, George. I knew I could count on you to keep up the family tradition. Well, what happens next is I have to get your exact weight and then do a few calculations. While I'm doing that, the costume department will get you fitted out with a full leather suit, a helmet, goggles, and ear plugs. Then you and I will go look over the equipment, and I'll show you how it works and what you have to do. How does that sound?"

"O.K., I guess."

***

Three days later we hear the ringmaster's voice: "LAADIEEESSS AND GENTLEMEN AND CHILDREN OF ALL AGES. You are about to witness the most death-defying, daring feat ever attempted by man!!" ... The ringmaster's voice seemed to fade into the background as the five-piece circus band broke into Fucik's *Entry of the Gladiators.*

In a dreamlike state, probably due to all the tranquilizers he had taken, George was thinking to himself, *Sometimes I get talked into the darndest things,* as he climbed into the mouth of the giant cannon.

This page left blank so you can write a comment about the preceding story

7

MI VIDA HA TERMINADO

The sounds of a flamenco guitar are heard, a Spanish gypsy woman slowly walks onto the theater stage playing castanets softly. She seems self-absorbed and unaware of the audience. She turns from side to side in a few slow flamenco movements, still without speaking. The guitar music starts to fade and then stops. The dancer stops as the music stops; she looks at the floor pensively. Then slowly she raises her head and brings the audience into focus. Finally she speaks with a distinct Spanish accent

"Men!" She exclaims with extreme contempt in her voice. "I spit on them!" *She spits to the side.*

   "My life is ended." *A pause*

   "Mi Vida ha terminado." *Her tone is emphatic and bitter.*

   'Flamenco has always been my passion. Since I am five years old in the Gypsy camp I eat, sleep, dream, and think only flamenco. 1 dance everywhere, and soon I am noticed. In dirty bars, at celebrations, in small theaters, I dance. First in Madrid, then Cordoba, Salamanca, in every city."

   "When I am twenty six I dance in all the most famous theaters in Spain and the critics write 'She is the one to watch.' Another says, 'Soon to be one of the great ones."

   "I have some small fame and begin to meet upper-class, wealthy people, and finally, Adolfo de Silva. He is very young and really just a naive boy. He declares his love for me and says life is unbearable when he cannot be near me. Soon, he is following me all over Spain like a lovesick puppy.

He has money and prestige, from his family's name. I allow him to escort me in public; it keeps other men from pestering me and interfering with my career. But with him, there is never sex."

"At twenty eight I am at the height of my career. One evening, while dancing in Barcelona, an American comes to my dressing room. He is an artistic agent. He says that if I go to America and allow him to be my agent, he will arrange for me to dance with the very famous José Greco. How can I say no?"

"America is as a dream come true. I dance with José Greco and we go on tour to many cities in the United States. Americans are wild for flamenco. Eventually, José Greco is offered a small part in an American movie and he wants me to be in it with him. Of course, he gets the main billing, but my name is there in the film credits."

"Then, suddenly, Adolfo appears at my door step. He is older and more mature now, but in many ways still a young boy. Again, I allow him to escort me in public, but eventually we turn to sex. I look forward to gaining the de Silva family name for my own."

"Soon I am pregnant, and at four months into my pregnancy I must stop dancing or lose the baby. I say to Adolfo, "It is time for us to get married.""

"My family will never allow it," he says, "Remember, you are of Gypsy blood. If I marry you, my family will disown me. I will lose everything. But I love you and want to continue to live with you."

"Of course, I am not pleased with this arrangement but I have no choice but to agree...until his mother comes to America and insists on seeing me."

"In a private meeting she says, 'If you love my son, you will get out of his life. He is young, and in the tradition of our family he can expect to have a brilliant career ahead of him. Marrying someone of your class, a gypsy, would be a millstone around his neck. You can never be acceptable to our level of society. Let Adolfo go, she pleads."

"I agonize over her words and the decision I must make, but then fate steps in and makes the decision for me. I am carrying packages and the stairs are steep. When I fall I manage not to lose the baby, but my hip is badly broken. I will never dance again."

"As my career fades, so too does Adolfo's love for me. Soon he is back in Spain and married into another famous family."

"Men." *Another pause.*

"I spit on them."

"Flamenco is gone, love is gone, all is gone."

"My life is ended."

And then she gives a final, anguished cry, "Mi vida ha terminado."

8

THE CHOCOLATE CAPER

The first note from the kidnapper
hA n d   o v e r A ll Y o r chockliT OR t h e Ki d gEts i T

The mother's response
Oh no! Please don't hurt my baby. Do you want milk chocklit or dark chocklit?

The second note from the kidnapper
What?

The mother's response
Well, milk Chocklit is bad for your teeth. Dark chocklit is healthier. Which one do you want?

The third note from the kidnapper
tHe Kid anD me aGre · e oN DaRk choCklit. THis aiNt A goKe So dont caLL the Kops. PLeSe.

The mother's response
O.K., O.K.! But please don't hurt my baby. How do you want us to hand over the chocklit and when will you return my child?

The fourth note from the kidnapper
PuT tHe choCkliT under thE S ocks in billys RooM ThEE kiD WiLL coMe baCk rIGht AftEr tHe pOwER RAnGers CarToON iS o · eR

The mother's response

That's too late.

The fifth note from the kidnapper

TheN *hOw* ABouT a*ft*er **sP**onge**B**ob Sq***ua***re pa**N**ts

The mother's response

You know you're not allowed to watch Sponge Bob Square Pants and besides, Billy, you still have homework to do.

The last note from the kidnapper

A*w* M*o*m!!

9

THE MOST AMAZING THING

The most amazing thing that ever happened to me was that I was abducted by aliens and held on the planet Nup for four days. And it was all my brothers' fault.

You see, my misguided brother thought that the pun was the highest form of humor. For example, when I asked him about my ability as a winter, his answer was, "Trying to write with a broken pencil is pointless."

He was so fond of punning that he gave me a tee shirt with an inscription on it that said "Have some pun today." That was the shirt that got me abducted by the aliens.

I was wearing that shirt one morning when, at about 6 a.m., I decided to take Fritzie, my Cairn terrier (think Toto from the Wizard of Oz) for a walk. At that time in my life I was living in the high desert surrounding Bisbee, Arizona. My walk with Fritzie that morning took us into a remote part of the desert.

Strange things can happen in the desert, so when we were suddenly enveloped by a dense fog I was not too surprised. What happened next is not very clear but it seemed to me that I suddenly felt very sleepy. Fritzie stopped walking and just flopped down into a deep sleep. The next thing I knew I was lying on the ground, too, and about to fall asleep.

When I woke up I found myself surrounded by fairy-like creatures. Each one was wearing earphones and carrying a small black box that looked like an MP3 player. One of the creatures, who, I later learned, were called "Nupsters," handed me a set of earphones and one of the black boxes. With gestures, the creature made me to understand was to put them on.

As soon as the earphones were in place I heard a voice say in perfectly good English, "Welcome to the planet Nup. Thanks to the new and improved model K226 Omni Intergalactic Translator we can now understand each other."

I asked, "What is the planet Nup? How did I get here? Why am I here?"

"You are on the planet Nup, which stands for New Universal Paradise. Look around you."

What I saw was a beautiful South Sea island right out of a Dorothy Lamour movie. The sand was white, the ocean was blue, there were coconut palms everywhere, and there were happy fairylike people all about.

The voice in my earphones told me that I had been transported to Nup by technology that was far too advanced for me to understand. The reason I was brought there, the voice said, was because of my tee shirt.

"You see," the voice said, "eons ago Nupsters developed technology that solved all our needs and wants. There is no disease on Nup. No one here has any unfulfilled needs, and we all enjoy eternal life. Having no cares or worries, or work to do, our civilization turned its attention to happiness and joy. For us, that means the joy of punning. Our greatest pleasure, and what we seek most, is puns and punsters. We have spent centuries searching all corners of the universe for them. When we saw your shirt, we decided to bring you here to test your punning skills, and possibly, to offer you eternal life here with us.

"What kind of test?" I asked.

It's quite simple, harmless and great fun. First, we will give you two days to explore Nup and get to know us. We want you to find out what our paradise is like. Two days from now we take you to our arena. You stand alone in the center of the arena, and Nupsters call out subjects to you. You must answer with a pun. It is what you earthlings call improvising, yes?"

"Just so," I replied.

I spent the next two days just wandering around Nup — it was indeed a paradise. Food was abundant and everywhere. The Nupsters were a happy, friendly people. I soon became obsessed with the idea of living eternal life in this marvelous place. With this goal in mind I began to rack my brain for all the puns my brother had dumped on me over the years.

After two days I felt I was ready for the test.

Here is how it went: on testing day hundreds of Nupsters gathered at the arena. I stood in the center anxiously awaiting the first "challenge".

A hush came over the crowd, and then someone yelled out "Noah!"

I snapped back with "I need an ark to save two of every animal, and I Noah guy who can build it for me."

The crowd greeted this with polite applause.

Next, someone called out "Dieting."

My reply was," Weight loss mantra — fat chants."

Groans from the crowd told me I was on the right track.

"Ink" the crowd called out ... a real challenge.

It took me a few minutes to respond. I said, "Why was the ink drop sad? Because her father was in the pen, and she didn't know how long the sentence would be."

This went on for eight hours. I was soaked in perspiration and I could hardly think, but finally, the test was over.

I was led to one of the grass-covered beach huts, given food, and told to rest. I would be given the verdict the next day.

The following morning, a Nupster leader came into the hut to announce that he had bad news and good news for me. The bad news was that I had failed the test and would be returned to earth. "The good news." he said, "was that Fritzie was going to stay on Nup and enjoy eternal life because she had passed the same test with flying colors."

10

THE HOTEL GELLERT—BUDAPEST

Dalebor Gorski was arrested by the Polish secret police in Warsaw in 1936. He was not arrested because he was a Jew, which he was not, but because the owner of the restaurant where Dalebor worked as a chef was a known anti-government activist.

Dalebor was found guilty by association and was sentenced to an indefinite prison term at a labor camp just outside of Krakow.

Panna Krol was arrested in the city of Lodz for stealing linens from the hotel where she worked. In 1938 she was sentenced to two years in the women's detention center near Krakow.

In 1939 Generalmajor Reinhardt Gehlen of the Wehrmacht was appointed chief of military intelligence for the eastern front. He was headquartered in Krakow on the estate of a Jewish industrialist who had "donated" his estate to the Third Reich.

General Gehlen moved his wife and only child to the estate in September of that year. He next requisitioned five non-Jewish prisoners to work as his household staff. Based on their previous work experience Dalebor Gorski and Panna Krol were sent to the general along with three other prisoners. Dalebor was to serve as the chef of the household and Panna as a maid and housekeeper.

When the five prisoners arrived, the general made it clear to them that they would be under the direct supervision of his wife and his aide-de-camp. The general stated that if the prisoners worked hard and did not try to escape, they would be treated well. Any wrong behavior on their part would result in their immediate execution.

Clearly these arrangements were far better than the horrendous conditions at the prison camps, and so the prisoners did their best to please the general and his family.

From 1939 to 1944 the war progressed badly against the Germans. During that time Dalebor and Panna fell in love and determined to marry at the first opportunity. Marriage between prisoners was not allowed under German rule.

By July 1944 the Russian army was within sixty kilometers of Krakow. Because of the sensitive nature of Generalmajor Gehlen's intelligence work he was ordered to move his headquarters to Berlin at once. These orders, plus the rapid approach of the Russian army, threw the general's headquarters into a frenzy of activity. Papers had to be burned, classified documents had to be packed, and transportation for the move of the entire staff had to be arranged, and so on.

In the midst of all this confusion the general simply washed his hands of his household staff. Making arrangements for their return to prison was just too difficult and time-consuming at this point. The general decided to leave the prisoners to the tender mercies of the Red Army.

When the Red Army captured Krakow in late 1944, Dalebor, Panna, and the other servants were arrested as collaborators with the German Army and sent to a military prison in Warsaw. It took two years for their prison records to be found and expunged. Dalebor and Panna were given work permits and told they were free to go. They were married on September 9, 1947. Dalebor was thirty-two years old and Panna was thirty.

Their first jobs under the Communist regime were at a two-star hotel in Warsaw, Dalbor as a chef and Panna as part of the housekeeping staff.

From 1947 to 1952, the political situation in Warsaw went from bad to worse. In 1952 Dalebor and Panna were given permission to immigrate to Budapest, Hungary, where conditions were somewhat better than in Poland.

They soon found work at the world-famous hotel Gellert on the Buda side of the Danube River. Again Dalebor was hired to work in the kitchen and Panna in the hotel laundry.

The local communists officials allotted them a small apartment on Vamhaz Boulevard on the Pest side of the river. Every day they would take the tram across the Szabadsag Bridge to their work at the Gellert.

Events in Hungary began to deteriorate and culminated in the Hungarian Revolution of 1956. While their apartment was not damaged in the fighting, a building just across the street was hit by a shell from a Soviet tank.

During these years Dalebor's resentment against the Soviet regime and its Hungarian puppet government grew and grew. At great personal risk he began to collect forbidden books and magazines, which he kept hidden in his apartment. From time to time he would take them out and read them, but he never became politically active. Panna took no interest in these events and remained politically passive for her entire life.

With the fall of the Berlin wall and the disintegration of the Soviet Union in 1989, Hungary was declared a free republic.

Dalebor, now seventy-four years old, was no longer able to work in the kitchen of the Gallert. Out of compassion for his many years of service to the hotel he was offered the position of doorman. He accepted, donned a long blue coat with gold buttons and a peaked cap with gold braid, and took up his post at the main entrance to the Gellert.

Panna, now seventy-two years old was kept on as the avowed "queen" of the hotel laundry.

The year 1988 was a banner year for Norman Kretzler of Omaha, Nebraska. That year he was declared the top Ford salesman in the state of Nebraska. As a special bonus from the Ford Motor Company Norman and his wife, Beverly, were awarded an all-expenses paid trip to Europe in 1989.

Neither Norman nor Beverly had ever been very far away from Nebraska, and while they had some concerns about all those foreign languages and strange food they would encounter, they were, by and large, thrilled about their first trip to Europe.

Their tour there ended in Budapest where they were put up at the Gellert Hotel. On the day of their departure, as they were leaving the hotel, Beverly whispered to Norman, "Honey, I think you're supposed to give the doorman a tip." Norman said, "Oh yeah," and he reached for his wallet. He took out a bill and said to Dalebor, "Here you go, old fella, you're gonna like this. This is real money." And he handed Dalebor one American dollar.

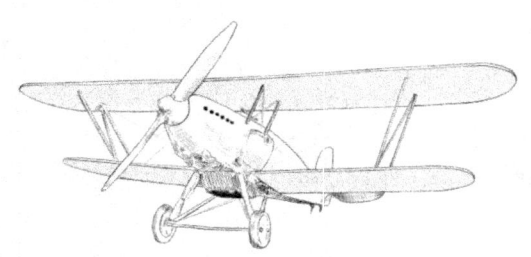

11

CONTACT

The pilot put on his leather helmet, pulled the goggles down over his eyes, looked out over the engine cowling of his biwing airplane, and shouted "Contact."

With this word Corporal Frederico Aquino of the Revolutionary Army of General José Gonzalo Escobar grasped the wooden propeller with some trepidation (he was still afraid of the big engine and its whirling propeller) and pulled it through a quarter turn. The engine coughed, sputtered, finally caught, and began to spin at furious speed on its own.

Thus began the first flight of an American citizen, working for a foreign entity, to bomb the United States of America.

The date was March 31, 1929, and it had all started a few days earlier in a saloon in Bisbee, Arizona.

Sitting in one of the infamous saloon and pleasure houses in Bisbee's notorious Brewery Gulch the pilot, Patrick Murphy, was desperately trying to think of some way to raise enough money to pay his bar bill, enjoy the benefits of a local establishment, and still have enough money to buy some gasoline to fly his biplane out of that miserable old mining town.

Murphy had flown his airplane into this part of southeastern Arizona a week or so earlier. It took only a couple of days for Murphy to persuade some of the locals to pay two dollars for a ride in his airplane. Now that source of money had dried up, and Murphy was broke and out of gas.

On the barstool next to him was his recent acquaintance and amicable drinking pal, John Stinson, owner of the Mining Supply & Hardware store in Bisbee. Noticing Murphy's glumness, Stinson mentioned that some of the locals were going to the Mexican border, just outside of town, to watch the revolution going on down there.

"Let's go have a look," Stinson said. "It might be fun, and it's free."

Murphy agreed, and he and Stinson piled into an old truck with some of the other salon patrons. They drove the mile or so to the Mexican border.

What they went to see was the revolution against Mexican president Emilio Portes Gil. General Escobar had started the revolution a short while ago and at the moment, was attacking the border town of Naco, Sonora, Mexico, just across the border from Naco, Arizona, USA.

Let me explain these double names. They go back to 1853, with the signing of the Gadsen Treaty, a land- purchase agreement that set the border between Mexico and the Arizona Territory. As chance would have it, the new border ran right through the center of a small old Mexican town. Officials on both sides of the new border agreed to rename the two new towns by taking the last two letters from the word Arizona i.e., *NA*, and the last two letters from the word Mexico i.e., *CO.* So there is now a Naco, Sonora, Mexico, and a Naco, Arizona, USA. Naco, Arizona is a mile or so outside of the mining town of Bisbee, Arizona. It is a de facto suburb of Bisbee.

The revolution of General Escobar had reached a stalemate at the town of Naco, Sonora. The general's revolutionary troops had surrounded the town and held the Mexican army garrison there under siege. Neither side was able to mount a decisive attack.

By the beginning of March 1929 the revolution had become a spectator sport for Bisbee residents. Many of them went down to watch the revolution while sitting atop railroad boxcars parked at a siding on the Arizona side of the border.

When the truck carrying Murphy, Stinson, and the others arrived at the border they all clambered on to a boxcar to watch the fun. The occasional stray bullet from across the border only added to the excitement.

Sitting up there on the boxcar, watching the battle, Murphy had a sudden inspiration as to how to solve his money problems. He would offer his services to the revolutionaries—for a fat fee!

Two days later, Murphy stood before General Escobar and laid out his plan. Here was the breakthrough the general had been waiting for, and he soon agreed to Murphy's plan. There followed a period of negotiations to arrive at Murphy's fee. Murphy had started with a figure of three thousand dollars. In traditional Mexican market style the general made a counteroffer and after much give and take, a figure was agreed upon.

The agreement stated that Murphy was to go back to Bisbee, and with the help of his friend Stinson, he would manufacture three bombs. He would then fly to the Mexican side of the border, show the general the bombs, receive partial payment for the mission, and then take off and drop the bombs on the federal troops in Naco, Sonora. Following the bombing, Murphy was to land again in the general's territory and receive his final payment.

Working in Stinson's Hardware store Murphy and Stinson made three bombs out of iron pipes and filled them with dynamite, scrap iron, nails, and bolts. For ease of handling, the bombs were put into old leather suitcases.

Murphy's first bombing attempt was made on March 31, 1929. He flew over Naco, Sonora, and dropped two of the bombs. Much to General Escobar's dismay both bombs failed to explode. Murphy landed his plane and said, "Not to worry." He just needed to make a small adjustment to the remaining bomb, and "everything would be okay."

Murphy tinkered with the third bomb and made his second bombing run on April 1, 1929. The second run was more successful in that the bomb did explode when dropped. Unfortunately, rather than hitting the federal troops, this bomb hit the Customs House on the Mexican side of the border and did no more damage than to spray debris on the Bisbee folks watching the revolution from the U.S. side of the border.

Undaunted, Murphy and Stinson made four more of the new and improved model of the bomb. These were dropped on April 4 and 6. The first bomb hit a trench and killed two soldiers of the Mexican army. The other three bombs landed on the Arizona side of the border hitting various buildings in Naco, Arizona.

The first history-making bombing of American soil by a U.S. citizen, working for a foreign entity, had been carried out.

The day after the last bomb run, on April 7, 1929, U.S. Army troops arrived on the scene and disabled Murphy's airplane. Murphy escaped to the safety of the rebel troops in Mexico. Shortly thereafter, when General Escobar's revolution collapsed, Murphy crossed back into Arizona and was briefly jailed for his violation of U.S. neutrality laws.

Following his release from jail Patrick Murphy faded into the shadows of history and was never heard from again.

Author's note:
General Escobar's revolution and Patrick Murphy's bombing of Naco, Mexico, and Naco, Arizona, are historical facts.
Frederico Aquino and John Stinson are fictional characters.
One of the bombs that landed in Naco, Arizona did not explode. It is on display in the Bisbee Mining Museum in Bisbee, Arizona.

12

THE GREAT BISBEE HULLABALOO

Author's note. This is a work of fiction. The town of Bisbee, Arizona is a real town and the events depicted here have not happened ... yet. But Bisbee, being Bisbee, they could happen at any time. Though the persons depicted here are fictitious, they all have real life counterparts in Bisbee.

The events I have described could only happen in a town as unique as Bisbee. In 2000, the American Association of Retired Persons labeled Bisbee as one of the "quirkiest" towns in America, to which I would add wacky, strikingly unconventional, bizarre, hilariously funny, just to the left of Sen. Bernie Sanders and just to the Right of Carl Rove.

Bisbee is located just over one mile from the Mexican border in the Mule Mountains of South Eastern Arizona. Its elevation is 5,280 feet. It is completely surrounded and isolated by the Chihuahua desert. Founded in 1880, it was once the largest copper mining town in the United States with a population of about ten thousand not including the residents of the eighteen bordellos located in Brewery Gulch. The decline of the mining industry in the 1960s caused the housing market to collapse which, in turn, led to a vast immigration of hippies and artists who snatched up empty miner's shacks for $1200 – furnished.

The copper mines closed in 1970. In the 1980s a new wave of immigrants, mostly university-faculty-dropouts, environmentalists, LGBTs (Lesbian, Gay, Bisexual, Transgender) and more artists, drawn by the magnificent scenery, pure mountain air and freewheeling lifestyle, settled in town.

As a consequence of the history cited above, Bisbee now can be said to be occupied by three cohorts, viz., The Miners (ultraconservatives), The Hippies (who never vote anyhow) and the Universityites (ultra liberals).

`Never the three shall meet.

Which, of course, led to the Great Bisbee Hullabaloo over the issue of tourism.

Hungry for tourist's and tax dollars the City Council and the Chamber of Commerce, backed by The Miners, were about to embark on an advertising campaign to lure tourist buses, which were already stopping in Tombstone, to Bisbee. Since this cohort controlled all the elected positions in Bisbee and the newspaper, they seemed to have the upper hand.

Leading individuals from the Hippies and the Universityites held a meeting in the old schoolhouse (now converted into artist's studios) to devise a counter strategy. "O.K.," they said. "If the Miners want tourists to see Bisbee, let's show them the real Bisbee"

The Peace and Justice Coffee House and Poetry Shelter is located just across the street from the bus parking lot. For weeks the owners had advertised free coffee and pastry for anyone who attended the Come As You Are Breakfast Party to be held at 9:30am to coincide with the arrival of the first tourist bus.

People began to drift into the PJCH&PS at about 9:05.

Walter and Jim (recently married) came in matching pink PJ's with feet and button flaps in the rear. Jim was carrying his Teddy Bear. A group of four women showed up in tank tops and men's striped boxer shorts. There were shorty nightgowns, terry cloth bathrobes, curlers and cold creamed faces. There were flip flops, bunny slippers and PJ's tucked into the tops of Doc Martin boots. A touch of glamour was added when Maurice, the town cross dresser, showed up in a 1930's, ankle length, satin nightgown with a large rose on the left shoulder and an open back that went down to just below his waist. Maurice was in full eye and lip make-up and dangling earrings but without his wig. He said he thought his bald head added a nice contrast to the nightgown.

By 9:30 the fifty or so partygoers drifted over to the bus parking lot. The bus was greeted with a chorus of "Hi, Sweeties," and "Welcome to Bisbee!" etc. etc. Some of the mothers on the bus covered their children's eyes. Others refused to get off the bus.

That bus left town at 9:45

The 2:00pm bus was escorted into town by a fleet of 1960's Flower Power VW buses. When the tour bus finally arrived at the parking lot there was a dense cloud of marijuana smoke over everything. A large crowd of tie dye, buckskin, Birkenstock wearing Hippies was there to greet it. A couple of the braver tourists got off the bus and were greeted with "Hey, man, you gotta try this. Like this is some really great s- - t. I mean, like, we are right on the Mexican border man. This place is like paradise man." Also on hand were the LGBT Choral Society and the Gay Men's Glee Club. Both groups were in full regalia including a number of large sex toys.

That bus left town at 2:20pm

The telephones at City Hall were ringing off the hook. The Mayor called an emergency meeting of the City Council. A town hall meeting was set for 8 pm that evening. A compromise was negotiated between the three cohorts. It stated that in the future all bus drivers would hand out flyers to the tourists asking the tourists to please respect the privacy and life style of the Bisbee residents and not to photograph, stare, gawk or ask to have their picture taken with residents. The compromise also included a provision that the City Council would never, never, ever, allow a McDonald's or a Wal-Mart to be opened in Bisbee.

13

THE BALLAD OF THE QUEEN MINE

"Oh, no! Not the railroad tracks!" shrieked Clementine.

"Sign this deed to the Queen Mine," hissed Simon LaGru, "or that will be your fate."

A train whistle could be heard in the distance.

"But I am a poor orphan girl, and the Queen Mine is all I was able to save of my father's fortune after you cheated him in that card game. You drove him to suicide."

"Such is life," taunted LaGru, "And I will have the Queen Mine or you shall die."

The train whistle sounded again.

"Sir, is there nothing I can say, or offer you, to dissuade you from this dastardly deed?"

"Ah ha," taunted LaGru. "Now I have you. Marry me and I will spare your life. We will share the profits from the mine equally as husband and wife."

"You know, as does everyone in Roaring Gulch, that I am betrothed to Roger Goodfellow. He is the love of my life."

The train whistle sounded again. This time, much closer.

"Sign the deed or agree to marry me. You hear the train. Your fate approaches. You must decide or die," LaGru sneered.

"Oh, if only Roger were here," lamented Clementine. "He said the trip to his father's plantation in Virginia would not take long and he would return with the money to repay my father's gambling debt and free me from your bondage."

"I see the smoke from the train on the horizon," jeered LaGru as he proceeded to tie Clementine to the railroad tracks.

Despite her struggles Clementine was no match for her tormentor, and soon she was bound fast to the rails

"You, sir, are not a gentleman," lamented the terrified girl. "Oh, woe is me. ... Is there no one to save me?"

The train could now be seen approaching at high speed.

"Unhand that girl you fiend!" cried Roger Goodfellow as he galloped up on his trusty white steed. "I have the money, and she is free of your clutches."

In a single leap Roger jumped from his horse and freed Clementine just as the train roared past.

"Curses! Foiled again!" bemoaned LaGru as he slunked off, exiting the stage, as the curtain came down to the roar and applause of the audience.

14

DEPORTATION

It was three thirty in the morning on July 12, 1917, when William Danaher, Michael O'Malley and Sean Riley rose from their beds in Mary Sinclair's rooming house in Bisbee, Arizona. The three miners dressed in silence and left the house without saying a word. They assembled on the small terrace in front of Mrs. Sinclair's house. The terrace, high up on the north side of the canyon that formed Bisbee's main street, gave them a good overview of the sleeping town. The only lights to be seen were from the saloons and brothels in Brewery Gulch on the western edge of town.

The three men lit cigarettes, inhaled deeply and, with a word from Danaher, set off down the steep stairs that led to the bottom of the canyon. Once down on Main Street, the men walked in single file, keeping to the shadows and doorways of the shops. They were headed for the explosives storage shed of the Phelps Dodge mining company just outside of town.

In addition to working in the copper mines the three men were "operatives" of the Industrial Workers of the World (IWW) local number 800 in Bisbee. That morning, in support of miners who had been on strike against the mining company for two weeks, the three operatives were intent on stealing some dynamite from the mine storage shed and setting off an explosion outside the main entrance to the Phelps Dodge office building. The explosion was not meant to cause any significant damage but rather to serve as a warning to the company.

When the men reached the mine site they climbed a tall fence close to the explosive shed. Staying to the shadows they worked their way around to the front door of the shed. As O'Malley was about to force the lock on the door a voice called out "Stop. Stand where you are or we'll shoot." The three men stood still with hands raised. A group of eight or ten men, with rifles and pistols drawn, stepped out from behind nearby buildings.

Lanterns were lit and the lights shown on the three operatives. "I know these three," a voice in the crowd said. "They're with the IWW communists." Then handcuffs were produced, and, with curses and rough jostling, Danaher, O'Malley and Riley were forced into the back of a wagon along with five or six of the armed men.

"Where are you taking us?" Riley asked, and as a reply, he was struck in the mouth with the butt of one of the men's rifle. "You'll soon see," someone replied.

The wagon left the mine site and headed toward the nearby Bisbee suburb of Warren. By this time the sun was beginning to rise. In the dim light Danaher could make out lines of men and a few women all heading in the same direction as the wagon. As the light grew brighter it became clear that the lines of men and women were actually being herded along by armed guards. "What can this mean?" O'Malley whispered to the others. "There must be hundreds of people being pushed along."

At around five in the morning the wagon turned into the old baseball field in Warren, and the three prisoners were roughly pulled from the wagon. Their handcuffs were removed. They were told, "Sit here and don't try anything. We are prepared to shoot to kill."

Looking around, the three IWW men saw that the baseball field was completely surrounded by armed men. "There must be more than a thousand men with guns out there," Riley exclaimed.

As the sun rose higher and higher in the summer sky the brutal Arizona heat spread over the captives like a smothering blanket. More and more prisoners were herded into the ball field.

By eight o'clock there were more than a thousand prisoners and two thousand armed guards in the stadium.

Around nine o'clock a tall man wearing a sheriff's badge and a pistol strapped to his hip stood up on the back of a wagon. "Is that Cochise County sheriff Wheeler" someone asked. "Don't know," someone answered. "Could be."

The tall man told the prisoners what was happening. "The IWW," he said, "is a pro-German, anti-American organization that is threatening the safety of this town and the property of the Phelps Dodge mining company." The tall man went on to explain that Governor Hunt had telegraphed Washington, DC, asking president Woodrow Wilson to send army troops to Bisbee to maintain law and order.

President Wilson had refused to send in the army, and so this vigilante committee was taking matters into its own hands. Walter Douglas, president of the mining company, had not voiced any objections to what was happening.

The tall man with the badge went on to say, "All of you IWW striking miners and your supporters are going to be deported out of Bisbee, and I warn you never to return. The two thousand members of the Bisbee Citizens' Protective League, that you see surrounding you, are prepared to enforce this decision."

Around eleven in the morning, the prisoners were marched under guard to the railhead south of Warren where they were loaded into cattle cars provided by the El Paso and Southwestern railroad. No food, water, or toilet facilities were provided.

Once loaded, the train headed east across the Arizona/New Mexico desert into New Mexico. The train traveled for sixteen hours, covering two hundred miles to the remote town of Hermanas, New Mexico. Once in Hermanas the deportees were unloaded from the cattle cars and left standing at the rail siding with only the money they had in their pockets and the clothes on their backs.

Before the train pulled out, the thirteen hundred deportees were warned once again not to attempt to return to Bisbee.

The illegal deportation of the Bisbee miners was never pursued in the courts, and no action was ever taken against the organizers or leaders of the vigilante mob.

Author's Note:
William Danaher, Michael O'Malley and Sean Riley are fictitious characters. This story is a fictionalized version of actual events that occurred in Bisbee, Arizona, in July 1917 under circumstances similar to the ones described here.

15

THE LAST OF THE ROUGH RIDERS

"Yep, my name is Luke Chatsworth and I reken I'm just about the last of the Rough Riders that charged up San Juan Hill with Teddy Roosevelt in '98. On January 25, in 18 and 98, when the battleship Maine was blowed up in the harbor down there in Havana, Cuba, some of them Washington fellers said, "Enough is enough." and they declared that we was at war with Spain.

Well everyone thought that was the right thing to do but them Washington fellers forgot that American didn't have much of an army to fight the war with. Things was so bad with the U.S. Army that President McKinley put out the call for a volunteer cavalry regiment to go down to Cuba to whup the Spanish and free-up the Cuban people.

At the time this call came out, I was workin' on a ranch just outside of Prescott, Arizona, bustin' horses and mules and doin' general ranch work. Joining the cavalry sounded just about right to me and Shorty Chavez. Now Shorty, he was a Mexican, said he wanted to help free up the Cuban people all right, but he also wanted to see something of the world at the same time he was doin' that. Besides the pay the army was offering was better that what we was making on the ranch. So Shorty and me, we went into Prescott and joined up.

They put us and a bunch of other fellers on a train and sent us off to San Antonio, Texas, for training. Neither me nor Shorty had ever been much farther east than Las Cruces, New Mexico, so right away we were seeing more of the world that we ever thought we would.

When we got to San Antonio we found out that we were part of something called the U.S. First Volunteer Cavalry under the command of Lt. Colonel Theodore Roosevelt. Now Colonel Teddy, that's what we called him, was some kind of special feller. To start with, he had gone to Harvard University and so he spoke a kind of Harvard language that took us a while to get used to. For example, when he wanted you to move forward quickly, he would say something like, "Now hasten along there fellows, hasten along." He was sort of a dumpy man with a mustache and eyeglasses but he seemed to have an endless supply of energy. He was like a bull in china shop that never let up charging and running around.

We were told that Colonel Teddy had been personally responsible for the formation of the First Volunteer Cavalry and that he had even quit his job in Washington, where he was the Assistant Secretary of the Navy. We all thought it was funny that the Assistant Secretary of the Navy would end up in the cavalry. But there he was, and you could tell that he loved every minute he was down there playing soldier-boy.

The uniforms they gave us, which we thought were pretty dashing, but which turned out to be the worst possible thing for the Cuban climate, were yellow canvas pants, canvas leggings, and a blue woolen shirt. The hats they gave us were a sort of wide-brimmed cowboy hat. The whole uniform was topped off with a yellow bandana, which we were to wear tied loosely around our necks. All in all we looked just the way a bunch of roughneck cowboy soldiers were supposed to look. In fact, though, we had New York City playboys, Native Americans, Texas Rangers, some of Davy Crockett's kinfolk, ex-policemen, and a few old soldiers from the Civil War in there with us.

We were told that the army had rejected some famous people, such as Buffalo Bill Cody, Frank James, the brother of Jesse James, and six hundred Sioux Indians. So we was feelin' pretty special to have been accepted into this elite part of the U.S. Army.

Most of us fellers knew how to ride and shoot but we still got some training in military drills, obedience to orders, military protocol and such as that.

Some of us hoped we would get trained in how to use the saber sword, since that seemed pretty dashing, but the army would have none of it. Instead, we were issued 1892 Springfield bolt-action rifles. We were also given .45 caliber pistols and great, big, ugly, and dangerous-looking, Bowie knives. We felt armed to the teeth, and ready for anything the Spaniards might throw at us.

Little did we know that the Spanish soldiers, who were well-trained veterans, were armed with modern-day Mauser rifles that could fire off eight shots in the twenty seconds it took us to aim, fire, work the bolt of our Springfields, aim and fire again.

Our military training ended on May 29, 1898. That was the day we were loaded onto trains headed for Tampa, Florida, where we were to get on a boat to go to Cuba. There were 1,060 of us soldiers and 1,258 horses and mules. When the time came for us to get on board the ship, it turned out that there wasn't enough room for all of us. Only eight of our twelve companies were permitted to leave Tampa, and many of the horses and mules were left behind. All in all, only me, Shorty and about five hundred other Rough Riders (as we were called by this time) made it to Cuba.

That war with Spain lasted one hundred and fifty three days and was often described, by people who wasn't there, as a "splendid little war." That certainly seemed to be the case for Colonel Teddy. Not many people realized that his total combat experience lasted just one week, with only one day of hard fighting. He was later quoted as saying that, "The charge up San

Juan Hill was great fun!" He was also quoted as saying "Oh, but we had a bully fight."

Somehow, it didn't seem like much fun to Shorty Chavez and me, especially since Shorty was one of the 205 Americans killed that day.

From where we saw it, the charge up San Juan Hill was more of a series of rushes by the Rough Riders and other Army units trying to get to the top of that danged hill. San Juan Hill is very steep and the waist-high grass was wet that day, and about as slippery as ice. We Rough Riders were trained as cavalry, not as infantry, so the climb up that hill, under heavy Spanish rifle fire, was just about the awfulest thing I've ever had to do in my whole life..

At one point in the battle, when the our troops seemed about to bog down, Colonel Teddy came riding out of the woods and, when he saw his way was blocked by some slow-moving infantry troops he shouted, "If you gentlemen do not wish to go forward please let my men pass." With that, and mounted high on horseback, Colonel Teddy, all alone, charged the Spanish rifle pits. I remember he was wearing his sombrero with a blue polka-dot handkerchief as a hat band. When he charged that handkerchief flew out behind his head just like it was his own personal banner. He sure was a sight to see. (Later, we Rough Riders adopted the polka-dot handkerchief as our company emblem.) Seeing Colonel Teddy out there on his horse, all by himself, just made you want to stand up and cheer for him. It certainly bolstered our courage, and we commenced to keep on slipping and sliding our way up the hill.

It was awful hard going and just about when I though I couldn't go no further, I heard a loud drumming sound off to my right. Someone shouted, "It's the Gatling guns. Our Gatling guns." I remember thinking *Praise be to Mr. Gatling* . The sound of those guns, at just that point in the battle, seemed to be just what we fellers needed to lift our spirits 'cuz once we heard those Gatling guns we went at that hill with newfound energy.

Eventually, through sheer stubbornness and willpower, we reached the top of San Juan Hill. We got there just in time to see them Spanish soldiers hightailing it down the other side. Cheers went up all along the line and I knew then that we had won the battle.

I guess we done good that day, which I remember was July 1, 1898, 'cuz forty three days later, on August 12, Spain surrendered and the United States of America had won that "splendid little war."

16

THE BESTEST COWBOY THAT EVER WUZ

I shore hope no one was lookin' the day I tried to ride that danged bicycle.

Ya see, a cowboy ain't got much he can be proud of or that he can brag about. And I guess it was them three shots of Old Redeye that got me to braggin' in the bunkhouse one night.

I jumped up on the table and shouted, "I'm the bestest cowboy that ever was, and I can ride anything that moves."

"You're drunk," Shorty said. "And git down offen that table 'fore you hurt yourself."

"Well, I may have had a few snorts," I said. " But ain't I the one that rode El Diablo at the Tombstone rodeo? And you all know it was me that was crowned BC [Best Cowboy] at the El Paso Roundup the year before that. I'm tellin' all you saddle tramps in this here bunkhouse that I can ride anything that moves."

Some of them fellers allowed as how I was maybe a pretty good cowboy at that. So with these acknowledgements of my superior cowboyness, and them three shots of Old Redeye, I was feelin' pretty good. I was about to climb down offen the table when Waco said, "If you're so danged good, how come you ain't rode that bicycle that's leaning up against the barn?"

"What?" sez I.

"A bicycle? Why hell, everyone knows a bicycle don't count fer nothin'. No self-respecting cowboy would be caught dead ridin' a bicycle," I said, with a superior look around the bunkhouse. But I could see that some of the fellers was looking doubtful.

I heard someone whisper, "Talks big don't he?"

I hitched up my britches, got down off the table, and headed for my bunk. "Bicycle," I snorted, and called it a night.

Dear friends I got to admit that, after that night, my ego was about as low as a rattlesnake's belly in a road rut. Every time I went past the barn, there that thing was, just daring me to try and ride it. Finally, I couldn't stand it no longer. So one evening just about supper time, when all the other hands were at the dinner table, I decided to show that bicycle who was top hand around this outfit.

I took aholt of that contraption and walked it around to the back side of the barn. Oh, he creaked and squeaked a bit, sort of like any unbroken horse will do, but I've handled enough horses to know not to be intimidated by that kind of stuff. When we got around behind the barn, I stopped for a few minutes to look him over and give him a chance to calm down before I mounted up. True, he only had two legs instead of four, but I reckoned he would be stable enough, so I mounted up. *Kabam!* . . . No sooner had I hit the saddle when he threw me to the ground. . . . Three times in a row!

Sure, my pride was hurt a bit, but I ain't nothin' if I ain't stubborn, and by the fourth time I mounted him I was beginning to get the feel of him. I figured out that if I pushed the pedals just a bit, it was easier to stay upright. We even began to move ahead a little.

Well, now, this is more like it, I thought. *I'll bet . . . . Uh oh, uh oh, he's startin' to trot down this here hill.* Pulling back on the handle bars didn't do no good in getting him to slow down. In fact, he was going at a full-out gallop.

Down the hill we went, right through Ms. Bailey's vegetable patch with tomatoes and string beans flying every which a-way. We sideswiped the chicken coop in a cloud of feathers, chickens squawkin' and runnin' in every direction. I do believe one of them died of a heart attack. Straight ahead was the water trough. *Well, at least that will stop this beast,* I thought. And then I realized that the water trough was right next to the pig pen!

Well folks, the water trough stopped the bicycle all right, but it gave that danged contraption one last chance to throw me, right over the fence, and into six inches of pig poo.

I gathered myself up and went around to inspect the bicycle. His front wheel was all bent out of shape, and he was hissing air out of his front tire. I could see right off it was a fatal injury, so I did what every good cowboy knows to do when his mount has gone lame. I took out my six-shooter and put him out of his misery.

17

QUINCY

You probably can't tell by looking at me now, but in my much younger days I spent fifteen years cowboying all over the Southwest. For ten of those years, I had a partner by the name of Quincy Adams. Me and Quincy cowboyed in Montana, Wyoming, Colorado, New Mexico, Arizona, and even down into Texas. We cowboyed in the winter in blizzards and frozen rivers and in the summer with floods and mud. We rode horses that were so mean all they wanted to do was buck you off as soon as you got up on 'em. Some horses were so dumb they couldn't tell the difference between a cow and a rattlesnake.

There was always a bull or two who wanted to gore ya. There were cows that wandered off into the cactus so you had to go in there after 'em and bring 'em back to the herd.

There's not much room for luggage on the trail. A clean shirt and a pair of dry socks was about all you could carry. And showers were hard to come by out on the plains . Most of the time Quincy smelled like a herd of cattle, but that was okay because most of the time I smelled like a horse.

When you cowboy with a fella for ten years, you soon find something you like about him. Quincy had a beautiful baritone voice, and in those days I liked nothing better than to hear him riding around the herd at night, singing in tha soft baritone to keep the cattle quiet. As for me, Quincy thought the beans, biscuits and coffee I made over the campfire were just great, like gourmet food.

Yep, we got along fine, Quincy and me. We were like brothers in those days. And ya know, just like with brothers, you can tell when a fella has something on his mind. So one night when Quincy rode into camp, I knew there was something eating at him. But ya cant rush a cowboy into anything except maybe the nearest saloon, so I figured that when he was ready, Quincy would tell me what was on his mind.

Eventually that night he did. He told me that he had decided to leave the cowboy life, and that he wanted to make something of himself other than being a babysitter for cows.

The next morning he packed up his gear and rode off toward town. I sure hated to see him go.

About a year later was in Las Cruces, New Mexico, picking up some supplies when who do I see walking down the sidewalk but Quincy. I could hardly believe what I saw!

He was wearing a great big, pure white, cowboy hat that had a dried-up rattlesnake skin for a hat band—rattlers and all. Around his neck was a silk robin's egg blue bandana and his white shirt was made of some kind of silky material, with pearl button. On the pockets of the shirt were red stars made of some stuff that sparkled in the sunlight. The hand-carved leather belt he wore had a buckle about as big as a dinner plate, with raised silver letters and the word *Howdy* on it. To top this off, he was wearing snow-white skin-tight designer jeans, with little red pistols on the pockets, made of the same sparkly stuff that shimmered in the sunlight. His jeans were tucked into the tops of white cowboy boots, with silver tips on the toes and more silver wrapped around the heels.

He told me that after he had left the cow camp and ridden into town he eventually met a lady. He became enamored of her and she of him. This lady told Quincy that she was going to start a dude ranch, so folks from Boston and Teaneck, New Jersey and such as that could come out West and get a taste of the real cowboy life. She wanted Quincy to be the chief cowboy host of that there dude ranch.

Quincy told me that as chief cowboy host his job was to see to it that the eggs Benedict was cooked just right in the morning, that the orange juice was cold, and the coffee was hot. And when these folks wanted to go for a ride, Quincy would stand by the horse and give them a leg up and adjust the stirrups so that they would be comfortable and wouldn't fall out of the saddle. He would then lead them on a slow walk around the ranch.

During his talk I was looking at Quincy and listening carefully to what he said. When he finished telling me his story I did the only thing a true friend could do to put him out of his misery. I took out my six shooter and shot him dead right there on the sidewalk.

Eventually, I was brought up before a judge, who, it turned out, had done some cowboying himself. I told him my story, just like I'm telling you, and what I had done for Quincy. He listened carefully to everything I said, thought for a bit, and then he said that what I had done was the most humane, loving thing he had heard in all his forty years on the bench. He dismissed my case as justifiable homicide.

18

THE BEAUTIFUL HORSE

There was a cattle drive working its way through Texas to the railroad up north. On this cattle drive there was a young cowboy named Hallelujah Johnson, but because he was so young the rest of the cowboys simply called him "The Kid".

The Kid was a good cowboy and always did his share of the work. But the Trail Boss noticed that lately something was wrong with him. The Kid was seen sitting in his saddle daydreaming, and he often let stray cows wander off into the sagebrush. All-in-all The Kid was not holding up his end of the work, and on a cattle drive every cowboy needs to do his share.

The Trail Boss rode up alongside The Kid and told him of his observations. "Are you sick?" he asked. "Naw," said The Kid. "I ain't sick." Then the Trail Boss said that he was going to rest the cattle right here for about a week He would give The Kid that week off from work to get himself straightened out. If that didn't work, the Boss would have to let him go.

The Kid lied when he said he was not sick, in fact, he had caught the deadliest disease a cowboy can get. ...The Kid had caught *the love sickness*. Specifically, he had caught it from Miss Annabelle Lewis, the waitress at the café in the small town the cattle drive had passed through a couple of days ago. She had served him two breakfasts, a lunch, a dinner, and an extra piece of apple pie. The Kid was totally taken with the love sickness.

His case was so bad that he had spent the last few days daydreaming about Miss Annabelle Lewis. She was why he could not concentrate on his cowboying. He had concluded that he had to have Annabelle for his wife, or life just wouldn't be worth living. So when the Trail Boss gave him this week off from work. The Kid decided that he was going to ride back to that town, make his love known to Annabelle, and ask her to marry him.

Now cowboys on the trail don't have many possessions because there isn't much room for luggage. A second pair of socks and maybe a clean shirt was about all most cowboys carried with them. The Kid had one prized possession and that was his beautiful palomino horse. So The Kid brushed his horse until it shined like a new penny. He then put on his clean shirt, saddled up, and rode off to town.

Like most cowboys, The Kid was not much for words and sweet talk, so as he rode towards town he got to wondering how he was going to pop the question to Miss Annabelle. Finally, he figured out how he could approach this in a roundabout way. He figured that if he were to ask Miss Annabelle to share all his worldly possessions, and especially his beautiful horse, she would understand that he was asking her to marry him. *Yep*, He thought, that was how he was going to do it.

When he got back to the café he ate two blue-plate specials. Finally, he got up the nerve to ask Miss Annabelle if he could visit that evening after she finished work. Miss Annabelle allowed as how that would be very nice, and he should stop by the house around 7p.m.

When The Kid arrived Miss Annabelle was proud to show him her new Victrola record machine. She even put on some soft music for them to listen to while they sat out on the front porch.

All evening The Kid tried to work up the courage to ask Miss Annabelle to share his worldly possessions but he just couldn't seem to find the right moment. Finally, around ten o'clock when The Kid knew it was time for him to leave, Miss Annabelle walked him out to the front gate, where his horse was tied to the hitching post.

When they got to the hitching post they could hear the soft music from the Victrola floating out from the house. There was a warm breeze gently blowing and there was a big moon shining up in the sky. The Kid thought that Miss Annabelle had never looked as beautiful as she did right then in the moonlight. The Kid knew that this was the right and tender moment to ask his question.

The Kid looked into Annabelle's soft limpid eyes and said "Miss Annabelle, what you would think of us forming an eternal partnership so that my beautiful horse would be our beautiful horse?" Now, Annabelle knew right away, that this was The Kid's way of asking her to be his wife. She looked up at him and, in answer to his question, puckered up her lips. At that very tender moment the kid leaned over and...

A few days later the kid rode back into the cow camp. The Trail Boss could tell right away that he had been cured of whatever had been bothering him. The Kid went on to being a good cowboy again.

Now if you were to ask him what happened out there at the hitching post that night the The Kid would simply answer "Not much." But if you were to ask Miss Annabelle what happened she will tell you that at that tender moment, The Kid leaned down and kissed his horse! Miss Annabelle could see right away where his true affections lay. So she turned in a huff and walked right out of his life.

And that was the end of that cowboys romance and how he got cured of the love sickness.

19

16.586 SECONDS

"Yep, 16.586 seconds. That's the world-record time for Cowgirl Barrel Racing. It was set two weeks ago at a rodeo in El Paso. I intend to beat that time. If not today, then sometime soon. This new horse of mine, Buddy, is the fastest horse I've ever owned. This is our first season of Barrel Racing, and Buddy's still learning, but he just loves it when we get out on that great big field and race around those barrels as fast as we can go. Three weeks ago we did the course in 17.788 seconds, so I believe Buddy and I can beat that world record."

"Well, Barbra, you just might be right. If anyone can do it, I believe you can," Jeanne said. "What time do you race today?"

"It'll be around four o'clock, depending on how the calf roping goes. That leaves me just enough time to go give Frank a big kiss and wish him luck in the Bull Riding competition. See ya later."

Barbra found Frank Jension at his trailer in the trailer park. As she approached him she thought, *Now that is one fine-looking cowboy. Tall, skinny as a rail, and tan as a nut. I guess I love him but....*

"Hey Babe," Frank greeted her. "Have you given any thought to last night's conversation?"

"Yes, of course I have, Sugar, but you know you've put me between a rock and a hard place. You want me to give up the rodeo life and Barrel Racing and go settle down at your ranch in Tucson, but at the same time you want to keep on Bull Riding all over the country."

"Someone has to earn us a living, don't they?" Frank replied. "And besides, you know I want us to have children as soon as we can. and lots of 'em. I know you can make a good home for all of us down on the ranch."

"Aren't you overlookin' the fact that I earned more money Barrel Racing last year than you did Bull Riding?"

"Okay, I'm old fashioned, but I firmly believe that a woman's place is in the home."

"Yeah, I know all that, Frank, but I need more time to think this over. Anyway, I just came by to give you this big kiss and wish you luck in your ride today," Barbra said, and followed that comment with a large kiss.

"Thanks, Hon, and the same to you in your race this afternoon."

Frank took the bull-riding competition and the $2,500 check that went with it.

The cowgirl barrel races started at 4:10 PM. Barbra and her horse, Buddy, ran the course in 17.905 seconds, just 0.319 seconds short of the world record. Her prize money came to $4,200. As she walked back to the stable where Buddy was munching a large bag of oats she thought *Sorry Frank, but Buddy and I are going after that 16.586 world record. I know we can beat it.*

20

THE NAKED TRUTH

"Are you sure you want to go through with this, Alice? Elaine asked. Turning tricks is no fun."

"I don't have any choice, Elaine. I've hit rock bottom, and I'm desperate. My rent is due on Thursday; my car broke down, and I've only got forty dollars to my name. Besides, it's only for a couple of weeks. That dream job I told you about starts next month. I have no intention of getting into The Game."

"Well, I'm glad to hear that. I've been hooking for eight years now and, like I said, it's no fun."

"All I need is a couple of hundred dollars to hold me over until that dream job starts."

"Okay, I understand. Now let me think for a moment. I want to get you started with someone who isn't weird or dangerous. I've got it! George Wilkinson! He's a nice guy. I've been doing him for two years, and there's never been a problem. I think he owns a small business or something; he's not married, and he seems to have plenty of money. Yeah, George is the right one for you to start with. A couple of tricks with him should get you through this rough spot."

"Thanks, Elaine, but I don't want you to give up any business on my account."

"Not to worry honey, I've got several Johns on my waiting list, so this won't cost me a cent. I'll give George a call right now and see if I can set you up with him."

Elaine went into another room and picked up the telephone. She returned fifteen minutes later.

"You're all set. George thought it was kinda strange, me calling him like that, but when I described you to him, he said, 'Sure, why not?' Here's his address. Be there tomorrow night. Eight o'clock sharp. One hundred and fifty bucks. Plan to stay the night. George will make breakfast for you in the morning. He's that kind of guy."

"Gee, thanks, Elaine, I appreciate this."

"Always glad to help a friend, Alice."

George Wilkinson had a fourth-floor apartment overlooking the upscale shopping and entertainment complex called City Place in West Palm Beach, Florida. Alice was on time, After two glasses of wine and an hour of pleasant conversation, it turned out that they shared some interests, they retired to his bedroom. As he got undressed, George placed his Rolex and a thick roll of bills on the dresser. Alice was mesmerized by the stack of money. *If only...*, she thought.

By 3:00 AM, George seemed to be fast asleep. Very slowly, and as quietly as possible, Alice slipped out of the bed and got dressed.

She was at the dresser and about to stuff the roll of bills into her purse when George said, "I wouldn't do that if I were you." He was standing by the bed and pointing a gun straight at Alice.

She spent the next ten minutes in tearful apologies and explanations of her desperate financial situation. George maintained a steely calm and was completely unmoved by her lamentations. When Alice saw that her begging and pleading were not going to work, she finally got up enough courage to ask, "So what happens now? Are you going to shoot me, beat me up, call the police? What?"

"Well thank you for those suggestions," George said. "But no, I wouldn't do anything so crude. Take off your clothes."

When Alice had stripped down to her undies, George said, "All of them. Take off everything."

Once she was completely naked, George led her out of his apartment, down the empty hallway, and into the elevator. He pressed the Lobby button. When the elevator door opened onto the almost deserted lobby, George pushed Alice out of the elevator. He then stepped back in and rode it up to his apartment.

The lobby was almost deserted, except for the Night Concierge, who just stared at the naked Alice expectantly.

"I guess you'd better call the Police," she said. "Nobody is going to believe me when I tell them why I am running around City Place, naked, at four o'clock in the morning."

21

JOHNNY ICE PICK

The summer of 1935 was a hot one in the Williamsburg section of Brooklyn, New York, and Johnny Adabbo was suffering from dry-mouth syndrome. He could only drink so much water, and it was never cold enough. Every day when the iceman, Mr. Costello, drove his old truck down the street, Johnny lusted for a piece of that lovely cool ice.

One day, while he was sitting on the steps of his house, Johnny started paying attention to how long it took Mr. Costello to carry a block of ice up to his customer's apartment. About five minutes on average. That's when Johnny got the idea of stealing some ice off the truck. He didn't want a whole block of ice, just a small piece. It didn't take long for Johnny to figure out that he needed a way to chip off a piece of ice while Mr. Costello was away from the truck. That afternoon Johnny stole an ice pick from the five-and-ten cent store. Problem solved.

From then on, Johnny always had a soothing piece of ice for his burning mouth. And he always carried his ice pick with him. It wasn't long before he was known around the neighborhood as "Johnny Ice Pick."

When World War II came, Johnny was drafted into the army, and on the assumption that cooks stayed far behind the front lines, he volunteered to become a cook.

Ice picks were always on hand in the kitchen. The U.S. Army considered an ice pick an illegal—and dangerous—weapon, but Johnny managed to carry one anyway. Known to his barrack mates as a sullen "loner" who always carried an ice pick,

Johnny was left pretty much to his own devices. That was fine with him, since it allowed him to carry out his small-time black-market enterprise selling stolen army food to hungry Italian and French citizens.

Discharged from the army at the end of World War II, Johnny returned to Williamsburg and embarked on a life of petty crime. Muggings, burglary, and the occasional auto theft became his stock in trade. Things became much more serious for Johnny when he used his ice pick to kill a man in a bar fight in a Williamsburg tavern.

Johnny's trial for murder brought him to the attention of Milton Grossman, the district attorney for Brooklyn. In a plea bargain, Johnny's lawyer got the charge reduced to second-degree manslaughter on the grounds that Johnny was a veteran with no prior criminal record. He was sentenced to fifteen years in prison at Rikers Island.

In 1957, Northeast Airlines flight 823 crashed on Rikers Island shortly after take-off from LaGuardia Airport, killing twenty and injuring seventy-eight out of a total of ninety-five passengers and crew. Shortly after the crash, department personnel and inmates alike ran to the crash to help survivors. As a result of their actions, then-governor Averell Harriman granted commutation of sentence to eleven prisoners for their help with the crash, they became eligible for immediate release.

Johnny Icepick was one of the men released.

His time on Rikers Island had served as a finishing school. He had used his prison time to build a network of career criminals, to shed himself of any social conscience he may have had, and to build a determination never to be returned to prison.

Upon his release, Johnny returned to Williamsburgh and a life of crime, this time at a much higher and more deadly level.

He let it be known to his circle of criminal friends that he was available as a contract hitman.

Over the next three years there followed a series of five murders in the Brooklyn area. All the victims were killed with an ice pick. The chief medical examiner for Brooklyn confirmed that the "modus operandi" of the crimes were all the same: an icepick pushed through the ear of the victims. The district attorney, was convinced that Johnny Ice Pick was the killer, and he sorely wanted to get his hands on Johnny once again, but despite the best investigations by the police department, he was never able to tie Johnny to any of the murders.

This was a good time for Johnny. Money, women, and drugs were readily available to him. In the criminal underworld however, the word was out that the district attorney was keeping a watchful eye on Johnny, and "contracts" for his services fell off.

No work and an expensive drug habit forced Johnny to return to petty crime to meet his needs.

One evening, in a particularly desperate state for money for a fix, Johnny went after the poor box in St. Francis Xavier's church on Sixth Avenue. He had not noticed Carmella DeVito sitting alone in one of the pews. As Carmella finished saying the rosary and got up to leave the church she was just in time to see Johnny breaking open the poor box. Johnny panicked, and remembering his vow never to be returned to prison, he put his ice pick through Carmella's heart.

Carmella was a widow who had lived quietly in her apartment on Garfield Place. Only a few neighbors knew that she had a son named Vincent. This was because Vincent had been away from home for the past seven years traveling with the World Wrestling Federation as one of its star attractions, wrestling under the name of "The Bone Breaker." Like most

Italian men, Vincent venerated his mother and had been faithfully supporting her for years.

It took about a week for word of his mother's murder to catch up to Vincent. By that time she had already been buried. Given the nature, and the circumstances of her murder, it was pretty clear to almost everyone in Williamsburg who the killer was, but once again, the district attorney was not able to tie Johnny Ice Pick to the crime.

Vincent arranged several private conversations with his manager, the owner of the World Wrestling Federation, and the federation's doctor. He got all of them to agree to his plan. After his next match the federation's doctor announced that The Bone Breaker had suffered a torn ligament and would not be wrestling for the next five or six weeks. He was going into rehabilitation at his fiancé's farm in Connecticut.

Several weeks later, Johnny Ice Pick's body was found floating in Brooklyn's Prospect Park lake. All the bones in both arms were broken. There were two ice picks found on the body, one in each ear.

After consultation with the district attorney, the chief medical officer for Brooklyn ruled the death a suicide.

22

LITTLE AUGIE

This is the story of how Little Augie Martorano became the Capofamilia of the Martorano Mafia family of Brooklyn, New York.

The first thing you have to understand is how names are handled in Italian families. If a male child is born and is named Augustus, which is a very popular name in Italian families, then that child will grow up being known as Little Augie. If a second child is born into the extended family, say a cousin, who is also named Augustus, then the second child will be known as Big Augie. The logic of this is that the second is a larger number than the first hence he is bigger. *Capisce?*

So in the Martorano family we have two Augies, Little Augie and Big Augie. Now even though these cousins share the same name they turn out to be very different people. Little Augie takes a serious interest in the family business while Big Augie turns out to be a straight, stand-up kind of guy who even takes a stupid job with the New York Port Authority, collecting tolls at the Holland tunnel. This, of course, is something of a disgrace to the Martorano family but hey, waddya gonna do wid kids?

The second thing you have to know about Mafia family names is that almost everyone has some kind of nickname...sort of a *nom de alias*. If you don't got a nickname fuhgeddaboutit; you get no respect from the family.

Now at the time of which I am speaking the Martorano Mafia family of Brooklyn, New York, is not one of your large Mafia families...though they are very respectable as Mafia families go. The Martoranos are putting the squeeze on twenty or thirty restaurants in their territory.

In a brilliant move that would be called "vertical integration" in normal business circles, they also control all of the garbage trucks in their territory. Of course the twenty or thirty restaurants are filling these garbage trucks with free garbage which is sold to pig farmers across the river in Newark, New Jersey for a very handsome profit indeed. With this and various and sundry slightly illegal enterprises, the Martorano family is doing okay. But like any business, they have got problems.

In fact the Martoranos have got two problems. The first is with the old Capofamilia, Little Aggie's father. It's clear to one and all in the family that the old capo is loosing his marbles. There is even a rumor that he has this here wadda call it..."Al Heimers disease."

The second problem the Martoranos have got is with the Costa family. The Costas have got big eyes for the Martoranos' territory and for the past year of so they have been trying to muscle their way into it.

So, like all good families what has got problems, the Martoranos call a meet-up to bring everyone to the table to discuss the situation. They even bring in the *consigliere* to advise them what they should do.

The two main contenders for the capofamilia position are Benny the Taylor and The Roach, who has this name because he looks like a roach. Both of these contenders get great respect from the family because they have each whacked enough citizens to make a serious dent in the population of Brooklyn, New York. Little Augie, on the other hand, is just a young guy who has not yet had no opportunity to whack even one citizen. Still, as the old capo's only son, everyone admits that he has a legitimate claim to the position.

At the family meet-up Little Augie stands up and says as follows, "Wid all due respect to Benny the Taylor and the Roach I am, as youse know, a graduate from Erasmus Hall High School. As such I think I have got the brain power to outsmart the Costa family. Therefore, I deserve to be the capo of this here family. If youse will give me six months, I will prove this to youse"

The consigliore figures this is a fair proposition, and Little Augie gets his six months.

Now, being a graduate from Erasmus Hall High School, Little Augie is a very smart cookie, indeed. He has seen from as much as a year ago what is going on with the Costa family. So to give him an ace in the hole, Little Augie has planted a ratfink inside the Costa family. He figures that with the information the ratfink is passing on to him, he will be able to outsmart the Costas.

His first opportunity comes when the ratfink tells him about a heist the Costas are going to pull on the Brooklyn docks. It seems that a ship has just arrived with a load of very expensive Argentine beef. The word on the street is that a truckload of this beef is worth a cool two hundred thousand large.

The Alabama Beef Packing Company has sent an eighteen-wheeler truck, driven by a local hick, to pick up the beef. This driver turns out to be such a hick, and so unfamiliar with the ways of New York City, that the night before he is to pick up the beef he has a tragic accident and falls off the Brooklyn Bridge while in the company of two gorillas from the Costa family. So all that is needed now is for the Costa's to send their own driver to the docks to pick up the beef. And who do the Costas pick to do this but Joey Bananas!

It is generally agreed far and wide and around and about that Joey Bananas deserves this name. Everyone knows that

Joey is not the brightest banana in the bunch. In fact, Joey Bananas is an ex-prizefighter who has been punched in the head so many times that his brain now looks like a bowl of oatmeal. If youse want some muscle put on a guy or if youse want some shoe leather applied to someone's face, Joey Bananas is your boy. But if you got a job that requires some brain power... faggedaboutit–Joey is the last person youse would pick.

On the day of the heist Joey Bananas is sitting in the cab of the eighteen-wheeler getting ready to drive off with the beef when around the corner comes a guy in a green uniform. On the shoulder of this guy's jacket is a patch that says "United States Department of Agriculture." This guy is wearing a name tag that says "Beef Inspector," and he is carrying a small case that has "U.S. Department of Agriculture Official Beef Inspection Kit" written on it.

The beef inspector walks up to Joey Bananas and says like this: "Youse cannot leave these docks without first I gotta inspect this beef"

Now this is very confusing to Joey Bananas, because nobody has said nothing to him about no beef inspector. Joey figures he has two choices. Either he can whack this guy right now or he can let him inspect the beef. On second thought, Joey figures that if he whacks this guy it will probably bring the U.S. Air Force or the CIA or the Smithsonian Institution down on the Costa family, which would not be a good thing. So Joey tells the inspector to, "Go ahead and inspect the beef."

The inspector goes around to the back of the truck and climbs in. About five minutes later, he comes out holding a dead cat.

"This beef is poisoned and I am impounding this truck forthwith. Also," he says, "since youse have been sitting in this truck for some time now the poison has probably seeped out from the back of this truck and is maybe killing you as we speak. If I was youse, I would get to a hospital right away and have myself checked out. Youse may be dying at this very minute."

This kind of talk throws Joey Bananas into a total panic, Since he figures the poisoned beef is no good to the Costas anyhow, he takes a powder at high speed and he runs off looking for a hospital.

No sooner does Joey get out of sight then Little Augie whips off the green cap and jacket and, badda bing, badda boom, he drives off with the beef.

It is not long after this that we hear that Joey Bananas has suffered a tragic accident and has fallen off the Brooklyn Bridge.

At the next meet-up of the Martorano family, Benny the Taylor and The Roach have got to admit the Little Augie has done good, especially since the Argentine beef actually sells for the two hundred thousand large. Once again, Little Augie stands up and says as follows, "Youse ain't seen nothin' yet. I am just getting started wid the Costas, and I still have five months to go."

His next chance comes when the ratfink tells him of a fixed horse race at Belmont Park that the Costas are planning to tap into. Here's how it comes about. The capofamilia of the Costa family has a daughter named Angelina, who youse would know as Angie. Angie is married to a guy named "No Shadow DePalma." He is called this because he is such a skinny runt of a guy that he does not even cast a shadow on the ground. For such a guy, there is only one possible kind of job, which is as a horse jockey.

No Shadow DePalma is scheduled to ride in the fifth race at Belmont Park next week. This race maybe, is going to be fixed. Entered in this race is a horse called "Paul Revere." He is such a dog of a horse that if there was a race between him and his jockey, the jockey would win by two furlongs. In fact he is such a dog the odds against him in the race are twelve to one. The owner figures to shoot the horse up with such a potent cocktail that he will make a champion such as Man O' War look like he is standing still. To be sure that nobody catches on to the scheme the owner has to wait until the very last minute before doctoring up the horse.

No Shadow DePalma arranged two signals to let the Costas know whether or not the fix is on. If the fix is on, No Shadow will adjust his helmet as the horses are paraded to the starting gate. If the owner has not been able to doctor up the horse, No Shadow will scratch his boot on the way to the starting gate in which case the Costas will not place no bets.

On the day of the race, No Shadow DePalma does not notice that there is a new attendant in the jockey's locker room. This is because the old attendant, just last night, suffered a tragic accident and fell off the Brooklyn Bridge while in the company of two gorillas from the Martorano family. So while No Shadow DePalma is in the shower the new attendant fills his boots with itching powder. On the way to the starting gate No Shadow is scratching his boot like crazy which the Costas take as the signal that the race has not been fixed. They hold on to their money and go home.

The Martoranos, meantime, bet the entire two hundred thousand large on Paul Revere at thirteen to one. This is a no-risk bet for the Martoranos, since the two hundred thou is Costa money,, anyway. Paul Revere wins by two lengths, and the Martoranos make a killing...figuratively speaking, of course.

Not long after this the word is on the street that Angie is looking for a new husband ever since No Shadow DePalma suffers a tragic accident when he falls off the Brooklyn Bridge.

At the next meet-up of the Martorano family Benny the Taylor and The Roach are about ready to concede the capofamilia position to Little Augie when he addresses the family as follows, "To give youse final proof that I deserve to be the capo I am going to administer the cup-de-grace to the Costa family. Next week I am going to steal two million dollars from the Costa family."

Now this is very big talk indeed, since everyone knows that nobody has never stole so much as one thin dime offa the Costa family. Here is how Little Augie pulls it off. The ratfink has told him that next week the Costas are going to New Jersey to appropriate a Brinks armored car that is carrying the two million in payroll cash.

A caper such as this is something the Costas are very good at. So we see that in the final act of this heist, The Baron and Bam Bam, two Costa gorillas, are dressed in Brinks uniforms and are driving the armored car to the safety of the Costa warehouse in Brooklyn. The reason they are wearing these uniforms is because the former owners are now lying face down in a ditch just outside of Sheboygan, New Jersey and will not need no uniforms whatsoever ever again.

If youse have ever driven to New York from New Jersey through the Holland tunnel, youse know that getting up to a tollbooth is like a scene from Dante's Inferno, what with twelve lanes of cars trying to merge to five tollbooths. The Baron and Bam Bam enter the fray.

They do not notice that a large black Cadillac, which, by the way, the New York City Police Department has been looking for for two days, keeps nudging them toward tollbooth number three. Eventually, they get to the window. As Bam Bam is about to pay the toll, the man in the booth, who is none other than Big Augie, speaks like this, " I see from the license plate that this is a New Jersey vehicle and that, as is proper for Brinks guards, youse is packing heat. Please let me see your New York City gun registrations."

"What gun registrations?" sez Bam Bam

"The gun registrations what New York City Mayor Michael Bloomberg sez is required as of this morning."

"We ain't got no gun registrations," chimes in The Baron.

"Nobody gets into News York without they got a gun registration. I will tell youse what I will do," sez Big Augie. "Out of my high regard for the Brinks company I will hold up this line while youse go over there to the New York Port Authority office. There they will give youse your gun registrations. It will only take a minute and youse will be on your way."

So The Baron and Bam Bam get out of the armored car and start to make their way through twelve lanes of cars toward the office. No sooner do they get lost in the traffic than Little Augie jumps out of the big black Caddie, climbs into the Brinks truck, and drives off with the two million and his cousin Big Augie, who has suddenly decided on a career change even if it means giving up his pension from the New York Port Authority.

At the next meet-up of the Martorano family, Little Augie is voted in as the capofamilia of the Martorano Mafia family of Brooklyn, New York.

It is not long after this that we hear of the tragic accident in which The Baron and Bam Bam fall off the Brooklyn Bridge.

23

ZIA EDDA

Vincenzo Albanese was born into a fishing family in a small town on the west coast of Sicily in 1911. His sister Josephina followed then came Annunziata and finally, in 1925, Edda, the baby of the family. From the age of fourteen, with just two years of elementary school, Vincenzo started working on the family's fishing boat. At the age of twenty-two he married Carmella Lotempio. In 1934, he was drafted into Mussolini's army. Their only child, Carlo, was born in 1935, the same year that Vincenzo's army unit was sent to invade Ethiopia. He fought in Ethiopia until Italy's victory there, in 1936. Disillusioned by Fascist politics and by his experience in the Italian army, Vincenzo, Carmella and their two-year-old son immigrated to the United States in 1937.

Vincenzo found work as a longshoreman on the Brooklyn docks. He paid a bribe of two hundred and fifty dollars to the head of the longshoreman's union to get into the union and remained a faithful member for the remainder of his working days.

The Martorano mafia family of Brooklyn was heavily involved with the union. From time to time, to earn extra money, Vincenzo would perform small tasks for the mafia family. His son, Carlo, now universally known as "Charlie", was raised on the edge of mafia culture due to his father's involvement.

Charlie became a full-fledged member of the Martorano mafia family in 1957 at the age of twenty-two.

When Vincenzo and Carmella left Italy in 1937, he promised his three sisters that he would find a way to bring them to the United States to escape the Fascisti. He was not able to keep these promises until after the end of World War II. Josephina came to the United States in 1947, Annunziata in 1949, and Edda in 1950. Josephina and Annunziata remained spinsters all their lives. Edda had been married in 1942, when she was seventeen years old. Her husband was killed in Libya in 1943 while fighting with the Afrika Korps of the German army. She was an attractive young widow when she arrived in the United States in 1950.

In the normal course of Mafia events, there were weddings, christenings, and funerals that the inner circle and ancillary members of the family were expected to attend out of respect for Little Augie Martorano the capo di capii of the family.

At several of these events, Edda had caught Nicky Piombino's eye. As a member of the inner circle, he made it his business to be introduced to her. Eventually, a romantic relationship developed. Not that Nicky had any intentions of getting married; however they made a handsome couple and soon became popular members of the inner circle. This meant many late-night parties, weekends at gambling casinos, days at the race track and nights at various clubs and bars. Edda succumbed to this fast paced life and, little by little, she fell into a serious drug habit.

Young Charlie Albanese watched the downward spiral of his aunt's life with a growing, festering hatred for Nicky Piombino.

When it eventually became clear to Edda that there would be no wedding with Nicky, she killed herself with a drug overdose.

Charlie vowed to himself that he would avenge his aunt's death. But how?

Prostitution was just one aspect of the Martorano's operations in Brooklyn. As the capo (boss) in charge of this part of the family's business Nicky had five "soldiers" under his direction. Together, they managed two salons (brothels), an escort service, and a massage parlor, using a total of twenty-four women. All but two of the women were undocumented aliens.

The U.S. Immigration and Naturalization Service (INS) was aware that something was going on in Brooklyn but had never been able to uncover enough details of the operation to make any arrests.

Three anonymous phone calls from Charlie Albanese were sufficient to start an investigation. After several weeks of staking out the four locations, some court-ordered wiretaps, and hundreds of clandestine photographs the INS was sure it had enough evidence to close down Nicky's enterprise. The INS raid took place just after midnight on a Saturday. By Wednesday, Nicky had been indicted by a grand jury. His trial lasted just three days; his sentence was twenty-five years at the prison in Attica, New York.

Charlie was satisfied that he had avenged his aunt's death. But now he faced execution at the hands of Little Augie for having broken the Mafia code of *omerta* the overarching, if unspoken, law of all mafia families.

Omerta binds a mafioso to absolute silence. Under it one must never, but never, talk to the police or any law enforcement agency about family business or family members. To do so is to sign one's death warrant. It didn't take Little Augie long to figure out that it was Charlie who had "ratted out" Nicky, partly because Charlie had disappeared shortly after the INS raid.

True to the code of *omerta* Little Augie set in motion a search for Charlie Albanese that lasted for two years. Eventually, they found him.

24

A DAY AT THE OFFICE

Little Augie Martorano, of the Martorano Mafia family of Brooklyn, New York, the Capo di Capi Boss of the bosses, and Don of the family came down for breakfast at precisely seven-thirty, as he always did. His mother had a plate of three fried eggs, two pieces of whole wheat toast, and a cup of coffee ready for him.

"Ma, waddya doin' wid three eggs. Ya tryin' to kill me wit cholesterol? I told ya, just one egg."

E sempre mangiare tre uona a calazione. "You always eat three eggs for breakfast," She replied.

"Please, Ma, just one egg from now on."

Sei sempre stato troppo magro. Si dovrebbe mangiare di pu. "You were always too skinny. You should eat more."

Augie finished his breakfast and got ready to leave. "What's for dinner tonight, Ma?"

Oggi e mercoledi. Sai che ho sesenprn fare cotolette il Mercolrdi. Giovedi eravioli, Venerdi e il pesce. "Today is Wednesday. You know I always make veal cutlets on Wednesday. Thursday it's ravioli. Friday it's fish."

"The Pope says we don't have to eat fish on Friday anymore."

Dio dice che dovremmo pesce il Venerdi, Che cosa fa il Papa lo sa? "God says we should eat fish on Friday. What does the Pope know?"

"Okay, Ma, whatever you say. I gotta go." Augie gave his mother a peck on the cheek. As he walked out the door he said to her, *Chio Bella.* "So long beautiful."

He went out the side door of the house to the driveway where Charlie Bullets and Jo Jo were waiting with the big Cadillac. The drive from his home in Sheepshead Bay to the "office" at Fifth Avenue and President Street only took twenty minutes. He walked into the office at eight-thirty.

The office was actually the back room of the Villa Napoli Restaurant. As Augie entered the restaurant, Charlie Bullets took his seat just inside the front door to act as the gatekeeper and bouncer. Jo Jo took a seat just outside the door that led to the office. Thus, two layers of defense were established for Little Augie's protection.

There were two desks in the office, a large conference table, a leather sofa and two leather armchairs. The desk in the corner of the room was the domain of Florence O'Brien, Augie's secretary/assistant and bookkeeper. Her desk was separated off from the main space by several tall filing cabinets and a work table. She controlled all of the incoming telephone calls. Ms. O'Brien had been with the Martorano family for eighteen years and had the remarkable talent of not hearing anything she was not supposed to hear and not talking about anything she didn't hear. She was well aware that her life, her big paycheck, and her future retirement depended on her discretion. One of Augie's "soldiers," who always carried a rather large handgun, drove her to and from the office

"Waddya ya got for me, Flo?" Augie asked as he sat down at the other desk.

"Johnny Icepick has been waiting to see you."

"Tell Jo Jo to let him in."

Flo pressed a button three times, activating a buzzer next to Jo Jo's seat and serving as the signal for Jo Jo to let someone into the office. Johnny Icepick entered and walked directly to Augie's desk. "Is it done?" Augie asked.

"It's done," Icepick answered.

"When?"

"Last night, about two a.m.. He was drunk, so it was a piece of cake. You'll read about it in this afternoon's papers."

Little Augie reached into a desk drawer and took out an envelope. "Okay, here's your other half," he said. "Listen, Johnny, the word is out that the district attorney is keeping an eye on you. So I am going to use someone else if I need this kind of service again. At least until the heat is offa you."

"Okay, I unnerstan'. You know how to reach me if you need me." Johnny Icepick turned and left.

About an hour later Jo Jo stuck his head around the door and said, "The *consigliere* is here."

"Don't keep him waiting. Let him in." Little Augie directed.

Out of respect, Augie stood to meet Tommy, "Irish", Noonan Esq., the lawyer and advisor to the Martorano Mafia family. The two men moved to the leather armchairs on the far side of the room and conferred in hushed tones.

"It's the Costa family," Tommy confided. "They have been muscling in on our territory for the past year. You gotta do something, Augie. It costs us prestige and money. Now listen, that ratfink you planted in the Costa family tells me they are planning a big heist of some Argentine beef right here on the Brooklyn docks. That's the heart of our territory, Augie. You can't let them get away with it."

"Of course, you're right, Tommy," Augie conceded, A hard look came into his eyes. "Leave it to me. I'll take care of it myself. I intend to teach them a lesson this time."

The two men embraced and patted each other on the back like brothers as the *consigliere* took his leave. Little Augie spent the next two hours in silence at his desk, devising a plan to thwart the Costas' heist. About the time he finished formulating his plan to take care of the Costas, Benny the Tailor came into the office Clearly excited about something. "We found Charlie Albanese!" he exclaimed.

"Where is that bastazo. I've been looking for him for two years," Augie growled.

"He's holed up on a chicken farm upstate, near a town called Westerlo. So what are you gonna do?" Benny asked.

"I'll tell ya what I'm gonna do. I'm gonna send him to hell. That's what I'm gonna do. You go tell Spooky, Fat Tony, and The Iceman I want to see them right away."

About twenty minutes later Spooky Jenkowski, Fat Tony Capolongo, and Iceman Strollo were standing in the office.

Little Augie, told them, "This is a very simple deal. Youze know that we've finally located that rat, Charlie Albanese. Benny the Tailor will give you the directions. All I want youze to do is find him, whack him and bury him. What happens between youze find him, and youze bury him, is up to youze. I know youze think Nicky got a bum rap when Albanese ratted him out to the DA, and now Nicky is doing twenty-five hard at Attica. So all I care about is youze bury him. *Capisce?*"

"Yeah, we unnerstan," Iceman answered for the trio. "It will be our pleasure to talk wid him for a while before we bury him." The three mafiosi left the office with a certain amount of glee in their steps and looks of enthusiasm in their eyes.

By this time it was getting late in the day. The last person to meet with Little Augie was Four-Eyes Scadudo, the family's accountant. After spending some time reviewing the cash receipts with Flo O'Brien, he spread several account books on the conference table. Then he went through them with Little Augie to bring him up to date on the family's financial condition.

"So, you see, Augie, our revenues are down," Four-eyes said. "This recession is hitting all twenty-seven of the restaurants in our territory. People just don't have the money to spend. On top of that, the maintenance costs for our garbage trucks have gone up. We're certainly not broke, but it might be a good idea to reduce expenses for now. At least until this recession eases up."

Little Augie was quiet for awhile, then he said, "Here's what I'm gonna do. First, you tell the restaurants we are cutting our protection costs from twelve percent to ten percent. We don't want them to go out of business. But be sure they understand this is a temporary arrangement— just until the recession eases up."

"Second, I want you to cancel that contract for the AK-47s. Things are quiet right now— and we have all the firepower we need."

"Finally, I want you to tell everyone in the family that this year's Christmas party is going to be in Atlantic City instead of Las Vegas. Explain to them about the falling revenues. They won't like it, but that's the way it has to be. And as for you, I'm setting the budget for the Christmas party at seventy grand. I expect you to hold to it. Got it?"

"I think you're making the right moves Augie so no problem on my end." Four-eyes packed up his books and left the office.

"Okay, Flo, that's it. I'm going home," Augie announced.

Charlie Bullets and Jo Jo dropped Augie off at the side door to his house. As soon as he walked into the kitchen, his mother said, *Tua sorella dice che sta per sposarsi!* "Your sister says she is getting married."

"Getting married? To who?"

Non mi dira. E meglio parlare con lei. "She won't tell me. You better talk to her."

95

Augie walked into the living room where his sister Carmella was watching television. He turned off the TV and confronted her. "Ma says you're getting married. Who to?"

"Johnnie Carrera."

"Johnnie Carrera! He's a baby."

"I don't care what you think. I love him, we're getting married, and that's all there is to it. End of discussion."

Note to self, Augie thought. *Have Benny Eggs check out Johnnie Carrera. I want to know everything there is to know about this guy, and then I'll decide if I'm going to let him marry my sister.*

Forty grand for the wedding — not a penny more!

25

STONY HINGE

Mafioso (*mah-fee-oh-soh*) Noun a member of a Mafia.
Spriggans A species of Fairie who function as guardians of (Fairie) hills and treasure. Spriggans are an infamous band of villans, skilled thieves, thoroughly destructive and often dangerous.

B. Froud and A. Lee, Faeries,

"We found Charlie Albanese." Bennie the Taylor said with an unpleasant smile

"Where is the little bastardo?" Little Augie demanded.

"He is holed-up on a chicken farm upstate. It's near Albany in a little town called Westerlo."

"You sure he's there? I've been searching for that *stronz* for two years," Little Augie said.

"Yeah, he's there, all right. So what're ya gonna do now?"

"What am I gonna do? I'll tell ya what I'm gonna do. I'm gonna see that he gets what he deserves for ratting out Nicky. That little bastardo is sitting on a chicken farm while Nicky is doing twenty-five hard in the Federal Hotel up in Attica. That's what I'm gonna do. Now listen Benny, here's what I want you to do. Go find Spooky, Fat Tony, and Iceman. Tell them I want to see them right away."

Later that night Spooky Jenkowski, Fat Tony Capolongo, and Iceman Strollo were standing in Little Augie's office, aka the back room of the Villa Napoli restaurant.

"Okay," Little Augie says, "This is a very simple deal. Youse know that we've finally found Charlie Albanese. Benny the

Taylor will give youse the directions. All I want youse to do is find him, whack him, and bury him. What happens to him between youse find him and youse whack him is up to youse. I know youse think Nicky got a bum rap and is doing twenty-five hard in Attica because of Albanese. All I care about is youse bury him. *Capisce?*"

Iceman spoke for the trio. "Yeah, yeah, we unnerstan'. It will be our pleasure to chat with him for a while before we bury him."

The next day the three Mafiosi were on the New York State Thruway headed toward Albany. In the trunk of the car was a twenty pound bag of quicklime, a large sheet of plastic, two shovels, and a Remington twelve-gauge pump shotgun. Each of the men was carrying his favorite "piece." They eventually found the town of Westerlo and the chicken farm. They parked the car about a quarter mile away from the farm and headed through some woods leading to the farm. About two hundred yards from the farm, they came across a small hill with a clearing at the top. Spooky Jenkowski went ahead to scout out the location, and see if he could spot their victim.

Fat Tony and the Iceman waited in the small clearing. While they were waiting, Fat Tony wandered around and after a bit called out to the Iceman, "Hey Ice, come look at this." he called out.

Ice joined him. "What?" he asked.

Fat Tony pointed to the ground and said, "Look at this."

"What, I don't see nothing'."

"Don't you see it? There's a perfect circle of mushrooms here."

"Oh yeah, now I see it. So what?"

"Well, it makes me think of that place over in Europe. Where all those rocks and things are standing in a circle.. I think it's in

Scotland or Bulgaria or one of those places. It's called Stony Hinge or something like that."

"Yeah, so?"

"Well, this Stony Hinge place is where they used to bury all those old guys."

"Yeah, so?"

"Well, we gotta bury Charlie someplace right? So if we bury him here, inside this circle of mushrooms, we can tell Little Augie we planted Charlie in Stony Hinge. Augie is a smart guy. He will know all about this Stony Hinge place, and I think he'll like the idea."

"Okay, if you say so."

When Spooky returned to the clearing Fat Tony explained the plan to him, "Sure, sure, whatever." Spooky agreed. "I spotted Charlie in the house. He's not packin' and I didn't see any guns around the place. Should be a piece of cake. So let's go get Charlie."

Several hours later the three Mafiosi returned to the clearing. They were half-carrying, half-dragging the semi-conscious body of Charlie Albanese.

"I never would have thought of burying him alive," Spooky said.

"Yeah, well I thought it would be a nice finishing touch," the Iceman replied. "So let's start digging and get this over with before he croaks on us."

"I knew it! I knew it!" Fergus said. "As soon as that fat one stepped into the circle, I knew no good would come of this."

"But what do you suppose they're up to? Surely, they can't know about the gold," Seamus replied.

"Look up there" Niamh said, "They're standing right in the circle and they're starting to dig. What else can it be but the gold?"

The three Spriggans looked up from their lair inside the little hollow hill. They were standing directly below the spot where the men were digging Charlie Albanese's grave. Of course, they could see right through the damp earth. They are Spriggans.

"Well, what are we to do about this?" Seamus asked. "We can't just let them keep digging. They'll find the gold for sure."

"They're only humans. Perhaps we can frighten them off."

"All right, I don't like the idea of letting them see us; I haven't been seen by a human in many, many years. But it's worth a try."

The three Spriggans rose up through the ground and stood inside the Faerie circle where Fat Tony and Spooky were digging.

"What the ..." Fat Tony cried as he dropped his shovel and jumped back about three feet. "Holy Mother of God," Spooky screamed as he tumbled out of the shallow hole.

The Iceman took a more pragmatic approach. He pulled out his pistol and started firing at the three impish-looking creatures. One of the bullets passed through Niamh, who casually ignored it.

Having regained some of his moxie, Spooky lashed out with a savage kick aimed at Fergus. His foot met nothing but thin air, and he tumbled to the ground again. The three Mafiosi then huddled together on one side of the shallow grave while the three Spriggins stood defiantly on the other side.

"Shoo," Fergus said. "Go away"

"Boo!" Seamus chimed in, as he made an ugly face at the three gunmen.

"*EEEkkkkkk!*" screamed Niamh in his most hideous voice, all the while waving his arms about and dancing up and down.

"They speak English!" Fat Tony seemed awestruck.

"Yeah, but what the hell are they?" The Iceman wondered.

"So what?" Spooky said. "There are only three of them, and there are three of us. I don't see no weapons on them. And we've got a job to finish here. Remember Little Augie said he definitely wants Charlie buried."

"Well, of course we speak English, and about a hundred other languages as well," Fergus said. "What is this job you're speaking of?"

Fat Tony had composed himself enough to answer, "We have come to bury this evil man here." and pointed at the prostrate body of Charlie Albanese.

"He's evil, you say?" Niamh asked.

"Oh yes, he is a very evil person. He has done terrible things to his friends."

The three Spriggans huddled together and spoke in whispered tones for a few minutes. Then Fergus said, "Well now, you see this is a special place to us faeries and we cannot have you just leaving your bodies lying about. So we have a proposition for you. Give us the remains of this evil man. We will take care of him for you, and you can go. That way no harm is done to anyone. You will have completed your task, and we will have protected the things we need to protect. Now what do you think of that?"

"And no one will ever find his body?" Iceman asked.

"Of that you can be sure," Fergus promised.

The Mafiosi spoke together for a few minutes. Finally, Spooky Jenkowski spoke up, "Okay, Shorty, you got a deal."

The next day, back at the Villa Napoli, Spooky, Fat Tony Capolongo, and Iceman Strollo spent an hour convincing Little Augie that Charlie Albanese had been safely put away in a place called Stony Hinge.

26

ONE AND ONE MAKES TWO

Joe Mazarek was raised in an orphanage in Pittsburgh, Pennsylvania. Despite his best efforts he never located his parents. Joe managed to get his GED high school certificate and stay out of jail.

In 1998 Joe, now 21, was flipping burgers at minimum wage and going nowhere. Anything would be better than this he thought, so he joined the Army and found a home. Ten years later he had risen to the rank of Sargent and was the squad leader of an infantry platoon. In 2008 he stepped on a land mine in Afghanistan and lost his right leg just below the hip.

Helen Wilson was a fun loving high school cheerleader from Dayton, Ohio. She earned her AA degree from a local community college and, despite her father's recent death, went on to get a degree in Psychology from the University of Cincinnati. By the time Helen reached 24 her mother had begun to show signs of dementia. Out of desperation, and faced with the rising financial burden of her mothers care, Helen joined the U.S. Air Force in 2004 when she learned that, as Helen's dependent, her mother's care would be taken over by the Air Force. Helen was given the rank of Second Lieutenant and learned to fly helicopters. Her mother passed away two years later.

In 2008, while on a rescue mission in Iraq, her helicopter was hit by a rocket propelled grenade and Helen's left leg was blown off just below the knee. Joe and Helen met at the rehabilitation center at the Bethesda National Medical Center in Baltimore.

Their friendship blossomed into a brother and sister-like relationship.

One day, after a particularly hard session of trying to walk with the aid of parallel bars, Helen called Joe over and said "Let's try something. Come stand on my left side and let me put my arm around your shoulder. Hold me around the waist. Now I'm going to lean on you and step forward with my right leg, then you lean on me and step forward with your left leg."

It actually worked. By leaning and alternately stepping they managed to move around the room. They both laughed and thought this was great fun. With practice they were soon making their way around the hospital and even into the cafeteria to the great delight of the hospital staff. When asked why this co-dependency worked so well for them they would reply "Because one and one makes two" It wasn't long before they were being referred to as "That One-and-One couple."

Eventually Helen came down with pneumonia and died after a two week struggle. She was buried in the military cemetery in Arlington Virginia. Two days after Helen's funeral Joe was found hanging in a linen room. The note pinned to his chest asked that he be buried next to Helen because "one and one makes two."

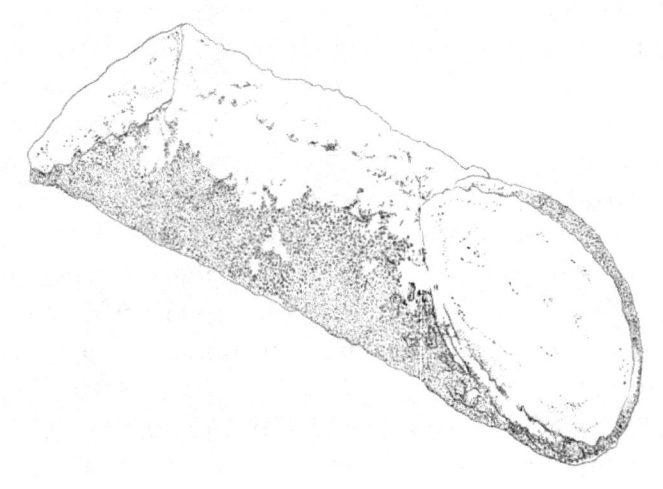

27

CANNOLI

Little Augie Martorano and Peter De Fillipo grew up together in the Bay Ridge section of Brooklyn, New York. They went to P.S. 163 on Benson Avenue together, and as teenagers, they played stickball every Sunday in the schoolyard. They had a long history as best friends. Things were going along normally until Peter De Fillipo fell in love at age twelve.

It was not a girl and, of course, it was not a guy that Peter fell in love with: it was cannoli. As is the case with every Italian kid, Peter knew about Cannoli before the age of twelve. But in that year, the gods of fate, for reasons known only to them, decided that Peter De Fillipo should fall madly, passionately and irrevocably in love with cannolis.

For those of you who do not know from Cannoli, let me explain. A Cannoli is an Italian pastry. It is tube-shaped, with a hard outer shell and a soft inner filling. The filling of real Cannoli is made of ricotta cheese. Most Cannoli are lightly and lovingly dusted with powdered sugar, and some have mini chocolate chips stuck on the ends. Cannoli are delicious, indeed.

Once Peter De Fillipo fell in love with Cannoli, he began to eat them all the time. He could often be seen carrying a little white pastry box from Callucci's Bakery, with three or four cannoli inside just to get him from lunch to dinner. By the time he was fifteen, everyone in the neighborhood had forgotten his real name and simply called him "Cannoli," or sometimes "Fat Cannoli." In his mid-twenties, which is the time I am writing about, Cannoli was on the low side of five foot two inches tall and on the high side of 250 pounds.

By this time Little Augie was in his mid-twenties, he had ascended to the patronship of the Martorano mafia family. Given Cannoli's dimensions, it was clear that he could not be taken in as a full-fledged member of the Martorano mafia family. Out of loyalty to his old friend, Little Augie made him an associate of the family, which allowed him to give Cannoli odd jobs from time to time.

When not working for Little Augie, Cannoli could usually be found at the race track. There must have been something magic in the ricotta cheese they used at Callucci's bakery, because the word on the street was that Cannoli was doing OK by the ponies.

One day, Benny the Taylor walked into Little Augie's office — the back room of the Villa Napoli restaurant— looking very peeved, indeed.

"What?" asked Little Augie.

"Ah, it's that old lady with the candy store again. She's three months behind, and I don't know what to do. You want I should bust up some of her candy cases or slap her around a little?"

"Nah, nah. She must be ninety years old by now. Besides, she used to give candy to me and Cannoli when we were kids."

Mrs. Birnbaum was, in fact, ninety-two years old, and she had been having a hard time of it since Mr. Birnbaum died. Her candy store was right across the street from P.S. 163, so she managed to eke out a living ... except during the summer months, when school was out.

"Tell ya what," said Little Augie. "Send Cannoli around to see me. I'll let him talk to her."

The next day Cannoli showed up at Little Augie's office. "Listen, Cannoli, I know we both feel kindly about Mrs. Birnbaum, but I have a reputation to keep up. She is three months behind on her protection money. I can't just let that go, or the other merchants will start pulling the same thing. So, you go talk to her like you did the last time."

"OK, I'll see what I can do. But you know that school is out and this is her slow season."

"Yeah, yeah, I know all that. You just come back with the money."

Cannoli walked into the candy store. "Hello, Mrs. Birnbaum. How's your arthritis today dear?"

"Peter De Fillipo!" (She was the only one who still called him by his real name.) "I haven't seen you in what—ten, maybe fifteen years. How's your mother?"

"No, Mrs. Birnbaum, I just saw you six months ago. Don't you remember? My mother has been dead for ten years. You must remember that; you were at the funeral. Listen, Mrs. Birnbaum, Little Augie sent me to see you about the money. You know you are three months behind, right? So what are you going to do about it?"

"What am I going to do about it? Blood from a turnip I can't give you. Maybe you could help me out again like you always do, Peter."

"OK, OK. But I swear this is the last time. And remember, Mrs. Birnbaum, this is our secret. Little Augie must never know."

The next day Cannoli walked into Little Augie's office and put the money on the table.

"Any problem?" Augie asked.

"Well, I had to dump over a candy jar and push the old broad up against the wall to show her she can't disrespect the Martorano mafia family. And that was enough, eventually; she came up with the dough."

That's the way it is with Cannoli—hard on the outside, soft on the inside.

28

DETECTIVE BILL

In the early 1950's, police dogs were just coming into use in big cities around the country. Not to be outdone, and to maintain the prestige of the New York City Police Department, the police commissioner decided that the department should get on the band wagon.

So one day the commissioner called the leading police-dog training center, which happened to be located upstate, near Albany. The commissioner spoke to the head trainer and explained what he was after. The head trainer said he would consider everything the commissioner had mentioned about the high crime rate in New York City and the especially dangerous conditions of police work. He promised he would think about all this and call the commissioner when he found the right dog for the department.

About a week later the trainer did call to say that he had found the perfect dog for New York City police work and the commissioner should come to pick up the dog.

The next day the commissioner and the chief of police got into their 1953 four-door Plymouth sedan, the standard police cruiser in those days, and drove up to Albany.

Upon arriving at the training center, after they exchanged pleasantries with their host, the trainer asked them to wait while he went to get their dog. He returned shortly with an English bull-dog and said, "This is Bill." The policemen were surprised since they had expected a German shepherd, or a fierce looking Doberman pinscher. But the trainer said that Bill was just about the best dog he had, and he was sure Bill was the right dog for New York City.

Now, it must be said that Bill was a fine specimen of an English bull-dog. He was built like a fireplug. All muscle from nose to tail. And he had that famous bull-dog stance with all four legs planted firmly on the ground like the ones you see on the front of Mac trucks. Bill had no neck that you could see; he had that pushed-in nose and droopy jowls that bull-dogs have and two large teeth sticking out around the jowls. He would have made a perfect mascot for the U.S. Marine Corps.

But more than all of this, Bill had a certain look in his eyes. You might call it a look of determination or resolve that told you he would not back away from any situation, no matter how dangerous it might be. When he looked you in the eye you knew he was a force to be reckoned with.

Based on the assurances of the head trainer, the Commissioner and the Chief of Police took Bill back to New York and, in due time, had Bill sworn in as a member of the police department with the rank of Detective. To mark the swearing-in ceremony, Bill was given a navy-blue sweater with gold buttons and his police badge pinned on it.

Two other detectives, Billy O'Brien and Tom Cassidy, were assigned to work with Bill. For the next couple of months the team did quite well. They collared a few "perps" (that's New York police talk for "perpetrator" which was how the police referred to all criminals) and Bill certainly did his part. Usually, when the perp was cornered, Bill would just walk up to him and fix him with that bull-dog look of his, and the perps would surrender.

Things were going well enough for the commissioner to assign the team to some of the toughest cold cases the department had been struggling with for more than a year.

110

One of these cases was the robbery of a very, very expensive mink coat from a fur store down at Broadway and Wall Street. After a full year of investigation no one had been able to break the case.

Detectives O'Brien, Cassidy and Bill went down to Wall Street to look over the crime scene.

At the fur store they met the owner, who told them what he knew and about the theft of this very, very, expensive mink coat. The three detectives looked all around the store and then Detective Bill suddenly grew tense. He got that determined look in his eye and very slowly approached the rear door of the shop. O'Brien and Cassidy could tell he was on to something. When the owner of the shop saw what Bill's reaction was he said, "Well that's right, we believe the burglar came in through the back door."

Most of you have heard of Wall Street, and you can imagine that the area around Wall Street and Broadway, where the fur shop was located, was a very ritzy area. What you may not know is that if you walk down Wall Street, away from Broadway and past the stock exchange, you come to one of the grittiest parts of Manhattan Island. And sure enough, that was where Bill went. Down Wall Street to where it ends at Front Street ... a very sleazy area indeed.

When the three detectives got to Front Street Bill hesitated for a moment until he spotted a pool hall just across the street. He made a bee line for the pool hall. Once inside, Bill looked around for a bit and then walked over to a rack of pool cues. He sniffed all of them and, with loud barking, fixed that bull-dog look of his on one particular cue. With that piece of evidence found, Bill went over to one of the pool table and jumped onto it.

What happened next truly amazed O'Brien and Cassidy. Bill stood at one end of the table with his nose right on that spot where the pool balls are racked up. He stood there for a minute, and then, all of a sudden, he began to race around the table, first to one pocket, then across the table to another, and down to the far corner to another. He did this until he had sniffed seven pockets, and then he stopped at one of the side rails of the pool table. He stood there for a minute, looking around at all the pockets; next he followed a trail from the side-rail to the far end rail and then back to the far-corner pocket. Clearly he had just enacted sinking the eight ball in a game of pool that had taken place a year earlier.

When O'Brien and Cassidy questioned the pool hall owner he said he remembered that it had been just about a year ago when a pool shark had come in and taken a local kid for two hundred dollars in a game of eight ball. He also said that the kid and his three brothers had gone looking for the pool shark until they heard that he had fled New York and moved somewhere down south. The pool-hall owner thought it might have been to Miami, Florida.

With this second piece of evidence the three detectives left the pool hall. They now knew they were looking for a burglar who was also a pool shark. Once outside Detective Bill picked up the perps trail again. He led O'Brien and Cassidy north along Water Street to a new housing development, South Bridge Towers, which had just been built right next to the onramp of the Brooklyn Bridge. When they came to the housing development, Bill went straight across the playground heading for the on ramp to the bridge.

He started up the ramp to the bridge with Cassidy and O'Brien following behind. They could see that Bill was moving faster and faster as he trotted across the bridge toward the

Brooklyn side. By now O'Brien and Cassidy were having a hard time keeping up. By the time Bill got to the Brooklyn end of the bridge he was running as fast as his short bull-dog legs would carry him. He began darting in and out between the cars coming off the bridge, and soon O'Brien and Cassidy lost sight of him.

They spent two hours looking for him but Detective Bill was nowhere to be found. When they reported back to the chief of police they were advised to wait for a few days to see if Bill might return. They waited for three months, and still there was no sign of Detective Bill. Eventually, the police commissioner gave up hope. After this bad experience with Detective Bill he had almost decided to cancel the whole dog program for the New York police department.

About six months later the commissioner received a telephone call from sheriff Bradshaw down in Miami Beach, Florida. The sheriff wanted to know if the department owned a bull-dog who would be wearing a blue sweater with gold buttons and a police badge pinned to it.

Of course, the commissioner said yes, whereupon the sheriff explained that the night before there had been a burglary at a pawn shop in Miami and that his men had captured a small-time crook and pool shark in the act. They had a clear-cut case against the crook, and he was going to jail. The sheriff explained further that when his men were investigating the crime scene they came across an old mink coat lying in a corner of the pawn shop with this bull-dog sitting on top of it.

The sheriff said that if New York wanted the dog back they would have to pay for the special shipping and insurance, which would cost about one thousand dollars. As usual, the New York police department was operating on a tight budget, so the commissioner said to forget about shipping the dog;

however he would appreciate it if the sheriff would mail him the mink coat, since it was evidence for a crime committed in New York. The sheriff agreed to mail the coat back.

About a week later, detectives O'Brien and Cassidy were standing in front of police headquarters discussing a case, when they saw a letter carrier, carrying a large box, coming down the street. Twenty feet behind him was Detective Bill, following him with that determined bull-dog look in his eyes.

And that's how New York City got its very first police dog.

29

LITTLE BOHEMIA

Norman, Oklahoma, was a pretty simple town in 1929. Most families' there-a-bouts had their roots in farming. The Great Depression had not yet hit Norman, but even so, a young farm boy such as Josh Askew had few prospects ahead if he stayed in Oklahoma. Josh and his family were quiet people who lived on a farm just outside of town. Josh had talked about his future with his mom and dad and even with his younger sister, Helen. In the end they all agreed that he would do better if he left the farm and moved on to someplace else.

Chicago had always fascinated and intrigued Josh so that was his next destination.

Chicago's booze, jazz, and gangster culture soon picked Josh up and threw him into a low-level, gang-related job, as a driver for a mob boss. For a farm boy from Oklahoma the life was exciting and the pay was good — until one night in May 1931. The assignment was routine. Josh and his boss were to drive to a certain location in Cicero on Chicago's South side, meet some Bohemians who had drugs to sell, make the exchange, and then drive home.

On the drive to Cicero, Josh's boss made it known that he did not like dealing with people he called "Bohunks." In his opinion, these middle Europeans were sneaky and treacherous.

This turned out to be exactly the case when, during the exchange, an argument over the price of the drugs turned the affair into an attempted robbery. Shots were fired; Josh's boss went down. The Bohemians looked into the car, saw Josh, and to ensure that there would be no witnesses, fired four rounds into Josh, killing him instantly. Andres Borjak was the trigger man.

The Little Bohemia restaurant on West Cermak Road was a favorite meeting place for Bohemian families...and gangsters. On Sundays, after mass at Saints Cyril and Methodius church, the restaurant was always crowded. The portions of savory pork, dumplings and sauerkraut flowed freely. Andres and his friends always visited there on Sundays, especially after Andres had become enamored of a certain waitress named Sonja Kovack. With a big car, money to spend, and a certain amount of European charm, it was not long before Sonja was in a relationship with Andres.

Al Capone, one of Chicago's most notorious gangsters, had only recently become aware of the huge profits to be made in the drug trade. It was inevitable that Capone and Andres should meet for a sale — this time in Capone's territory on Chicago's North Side. An anonymous phone call to Capone two days before the drug sale had warned him to beware of Bohemian treachery. Not one to be taken advantage of, Capone was prepared for the sale to turn sour. It did, but Capone was faster on the draw than Andres who took two of Capon's .45 caliber slugs through the heart.

The next day Sonja Kovack boarded a train at Union Station that would take her back to her quiet family on the farm just outside of Norman, Oklahoma.

This page left blank so you can write a comment about the preceding story

30

DUST BOWL DIARY

Sharecropping is the most common application of the sharefarming principle. In practice, sharefarmers work land which they don't own in return for varying portions of the total profit. In many cases where it is practiced in very poor farming communities, it is considered an exploitative model. Sharecropping began after the Civil War and ended between the 1930s and the 1940s.

Wikipedia: Share farming

Adams, Oklahoma, April, 20, 1931

My wife, Ellie, says I should keep this diary so that when our girls, Helen and Jill, grow up they will have it to look back on and be able to remember their childhood. We've been sharecropping these twenty five acres for two years now. The owner, Mr. Askew, is a good man, and he has treated us fairly so far.

Last year was a good year. Wheat was at a dollar fifty five a bushel and we came out a bit ahead of our expenses.

I have just finished harvesting the winter-wheat crop. The weather was good, and the rain came at just the right time. We got thirteen bushels per acre, but the price had fallen to a dollar ten cents a bushel. After the reckoning with Mr. Askew, our share was $1,110. Last year our expenses, for the four of us, were eight hundred dollars so we came out three hundred and eleven dollars ahead for the year. If we can cut our expenses this year, and if the price of wheat holds up, we should be all-right.

Jim Jackson says he will sell me a milk cow for fifteen dollars. It would provide milk for the children, and Ellie says she can make and sell some cheese. Guess I'll buy the cow.

Spring wheat crop goes into the ground next month.

July 25, 1931

No rain for eighty six days.

The cow is doing well, and Ellie is happy with her.

Henry, my old mule, died last week. Fortunately, the spring wheat was in the ground. I can wait until harvest time in September before buying a new mule.

August 10, 1931

Still no rain. The next 15 days are critical.

September 1, 1931

The new mule, Adam, is young and doesn't take to the plow very well. Makes for hard work.

September 6, 1931

Got a few sprinkles in late August and last week. Not much hope for this crop.

September 23, 1931

Disaster. We only got seven bushels per acre and the price has gone down to seventy five cents a bushel. After settling with Mr. Askew, I owe him five hundred and eighty seven dollars. He says he will lend me enough money for the seed for the winter-wheat crop. But he is limiting my credit at the grocery store to three hundred dollars.

Winter-wheat crop goes in the ground next week, if the rains come back, and the price of wheat goes back up, I should make enough to pay off all these debts; but, there won't be much left over.

Ellie is pregnant.

March 5, 1932

It's official, we are in a drought. No rain in six months.

May 10, 1932

Nothing came out of the ground. No crop at all. I owe Mr. Askew twelve hundred dollars. No credit at the grocery store. Mr. Askew says that since nobody is farming anyhow, we can stay in the cabin for now.

Ellie's garden will have to feed us. There's no hay for the cow, so she will dry up soon. Since I can't get any money for seed, and it looks like the drought will continue, I will try to sell the mule.

The soil is so dry, the wind is starting to carry the topsoil away.

August 25, 1932

It's a boy! Donald. Seven pounds, thirteen ounces. The ten dollars I got for the mule just covered the midwife expenses.

September 24, 1932

I butchered the cow. It was very upsetting to the girls.

December 22, 1932

This is a hard winter. I made up a batch of flour paste and papered the inside of the cabin with newspaper. That helped some, but not much. The school has closed for the winter. Don't know whether or not it will open again. With the girls at home and the new baby, Ellie has her hands full. I got some carpentry work for a couple of weeks, but no more in sight.

March 28, 1933

Roosevelt was elected President. He says that "the only thing we have to fear is fear itself." If he were in my place, he would know what real fear is like.

May 12, 1933

Wheat is down to thirty cents a bushel. Don't make no difference though, because nobody is planting anyway.

June, 1933

I have to give President Roosevelt credit. He got a law passed that allows the Department of Agriculture to distribute food to folks in need. Two times a month we can get three pounds of cheese, two pounds of lard or cooking oil, five pounds of rice or wheat, and three pounds of powdered milk. Not much, but we can survive on it.

August, 1933

The WPA is starting a work program on the county road. I've been hired for two months at fifty-two dollars and fifty cents a month. It will help to have real cash money.

November, 13 1933

This past year has been so bad, I couldn't bring myself to write much about it but something historic happened two days ago, and I feel I must put something down in this diary. Officially, they are calling it a dust storm. Since we have had no rain since October 1931, the ground here has just dried up and turned to powder. Two days ago, November 11, 1933, the wind started to blow with a fierceness beyond anything anyone here has ever seen. In the middle of the afternoon the sky turned black, and you could hardly see your hand in front of your face. The wind-blown sand practically scrubbed the skin off your body. The sand penetrated everything. It came through the cracks around the windows and doors and got into our food. Today we even found sand in the clothes that were folded up in the dresser. Someone said they found sand inside the vault of the bank when they opened it this morning.

January 11, 1934

Oklahoma and Texas are now called the Dust Bowl of America. We are still in a severe drought, and the wind and dust are devastating the land and the people hereabouts. We are living in the land of poverty. Families are starting to leave and moving to California in hope of finding work.

An unusual source of food has come our way recently. The drought has forced millions of rabbits to come down from the foothills in search of food and water. They have become such a pestilence that some weekends we have a rabbit roundup. At first we killed them with shotguns, but that became too expensive, so now we herd them into a wire corral and send young boys in with clubs to kill them. Last week I brought home fifteen of them. Ellie stewed and fried some, and I made jerky out of the rest. Not much, but it's food.

May 10, 1934

Two days of the worst dust storms so far. We were trapped in the house. Several people got caught outside and died. I am at my wits' end as to how to feed my family and keep us alive. I haven't been to church in years, but now we all go on Sunday. Has God forsaken us?

April 18, 1935

They're calling it Black Sunday. Starting on April 14, 1935, we had three days of a dust storm of historic proportions. I'm told it swept through the entire Oklahoma Panhandle and as far south as Amarillo, Texas. It covered thousands of square miles. When we looked out the window two days later, everything was covered with sand: the fences, the wagon, and half way up the side of the house. There was nothing to see for miles around but an ocean of sand.

April 25, 1935

Donald is having trouble breathing. It's called Dust Bowl Pneumonia. Very worried for him.

April 30, 1935

Donald is dead.

Ellie and I and the girls are leaving this awful place. We will follow the other Oakies to California and hope for the best.

31

A WONDERFUL GIFT

This was not the first time I had seen a leprechaun, but this leprechaun was unusual. Oh, he had all the usual accouterments— a clay pipe clenched in his teeth, pointy-toed shoes and a green top hat. What made him appear unusual was that he was carrying a shovel.

Now, what would a leprechaun be doing with a shovel? I wondered. I decided to ask him.

"Good day to ye," sez I.

"What? Can you see me?" replies he. "You're a human and you're not supposed to see me unless I choose to let you. What's the world coming to?"

"Yes, I know. It's a gift I've had since childhood. Other humans don't believe I can see leprechauns, but I can," I answered. "But I'm curious to know why you're carrying that shovel."

"Well, me boyo, if you must know, I've lost me pot of gold. And when I find it, it's me intention to dig it up and move it to some place I'll not soon forget."

"How could you forget something as important as where you buried your gold?"

"Well, it's something you humans don't know about, but timeworn leprechauns can begin to lose their memories just as humans do. It's what you call 'Old Timer's Disease' or something like that."

"And how old are you?" I asked.

"Two hundred and fifty-seven years old by human reckoning."

"That's amazing," I said. "You don't look a day over eighty."

"Thank you." he said. "But now I must be getting along to find me gold."

"Can I help you? I know the countryside around here very well."

He replied, "Ah ha! Now I see your game. Help me indeed! You want to steal me gold, you thieving rascal."

"Not at all, at all," Sez I. "I know all the misfortunes that can come to people who come into sudden riches, and that's not for me. I promise not to steal your gold if we find it. I just want to help."

"You promise solemn oath? Do you know what we leprechauns can do to you if you steal our gold?"

"Yes, I know."

"All right then. Let's be off."

Based on what the leprechaun, whose name was Shamus, told me, we started up the hill. As we walked, I pointed out what I thought were likely hiding places for the gold—a bush here, the base of a tree there, a large rock. But at every suggestion, he said, "No, no. Not there."

Eventually, we came to a small pond fed by a twenty-five foot high waterfall at one end and drained by a small stream that ran downhill at the other end.

"Hmmm," Shamus said, "this place has a familiar look about it." With that comment to spur us on, we searched the entire perimeter of the pond looking for likely hiding places but to no avail. In frustration, we sat down at the foot of the waterfall as we considered what to do next. Then I suddenly noticed a narrow footpath that led behind the falling water. "Shamus," I said. "Look, there's a cave back there."

"Faith and begorra that's it!" he shouted, as he jumped up and headed for the footpath.

Once inside the cave, it didn't take us long to find the large rock behind which Shamus had hidden the gold. He tried to lift the pot of gold but was unable to move it.

"I hid it here ninety—seven years ago. I was much stronger then," he said. Together we carried the pot out of the cave and into the surrounding forest. He soon found a small but sturdy oak tree that he said would be around for many, many years.

"The foot of this young oak tree will be the new home for me gold," he said.

Together we dug a deep hole and put the pot of gold into it.

We soon had the gold buried and the ground looking as if it had not been touched for many years.

Well now," Shamus said, "that's done, and I'm grateful for your help. I must think of a proper reward for you for all your help and for keeping your promise not to steal me gold. What shall it be?"

"That won't be necessary," I said. "Helping you was an adventure, and I'll treasure the memory of this day for a long, long time."

"No," sez he. "It's a reward you must have, and I think I have the very thing. You said your ability to see leprechauns was a gift you've had since childhood. I'm going to give you another gift—the ability to see faeries. Now close your eyes and clear your mind."

I did as I was told and in a moment, felt a warm shiver run up my spine, across the top of my head, and down into my eyes. When I opened my eyes, there they were — faeries of all kinds and sizes. Some were flitting about; while others were sitting in groups, chatting away.

One fairy in particular caught my attention because she was carrying a tiny bear cub cradled in her arms.

I turned and thanked Shamus, and in a hurried goodbye said, "Thank you for this most wonderful gift, Shamus. Now I must be off to find that fairy with the bear cub. I wonder where she's taking it?"

32

BACKSTAGE AT THE NUTCRACKER

"Oh *merde*," said Delphinium. "I dropped one of my contacts." She knelt on the floor and began searching frantically for the missing lens.

"Look at this tutu. The damn thing is falling apart. I can't go onstage looking like this. Wardrobe!" Marigold shouted. "Where are those god damn wardrobe people?

They're never around when you need them."

"You think you've got problems, honey?" Peony said. "I just split my tights. Come on; I'll help you find the wardrobe people." Marigold and Peony went off to find them.

The Dance Mistress entered the flower's dressing room and called for attention.

When everyone had quieted down, she said, "I want to remind you, once again, that the Fairy Queen is attending tonight's performance. Also, for this particular event, they have brought in two bus loads of elfish children, so I want you all to dance your very best.

Now please continue to get dressed."

"Elfish children — *retards*!" Wisteria said to no one in particular.

"I know it was you Honeysuckle. Don't try to deny it. I've seen you eyeing my new eye shadow all week, and now it's missing. Give it back," Delphinium demanded.

"I just wanted to borrow it. I was going to give it back anyway, so here. Some friend you are. *Bitch* Honeysuckle murmured under her breath as she handed the eye shadow back to Delphinium.

"Am I showing?" Morning glory asked Camellia. Both fairies were standing outside the flower's dressing room.

"Just a tiny bit. How far along are you?" Camellia asked.

"Three months."

"You shouldn't be dancing at all. You have to think of the baby. Suck your tummy in and let me look at you."

Morning glory did as she was asked then stood in profile for Camellia.

"Well, I guess you can get away with it for a while," Camellia judged. "But be careful when you do those etendres. You might hurt yourself or the baby."

"Listen," Petunia whispered to Wisteria, "you know that Moon Elf who works in the lighting department? Well, stay away from him. He seems like a nice guy, but he is all hands if he gets you alone."

"Yeah, but he is cute," Wisteria answered. "Maybe I wouldn't mind his hands all over me. Think I'll give him a try."

"You're a natural born whore," Petunia observed.

Having found, and completed their business with the wardrobe people, Marigold and Peony were using the peep holes in the main curtain to look over the audience. "See, there he is again," Marigold said. "The tall elf in the yellow tunic. There, in the third row.

He says he thinks this whole Nutcracker thing is weird anyway, but he keeps coming back. He says he's going to come to every performance just to see me."

"He is handsome," Peony responded. "And look at those long, lovely, pointy ears.

You know what they say about elves with long pointy ears; long pointy ears mean they also have a long well you know."

"You crowd me just one more time on the line, and I am going to scratch your eyes out. Do you understand me?" Snap dragon threatened Sweet Pea.

"If you weren't getting so fat, and could move faster, I wouldn't have to crowd you.

Dancing behind you is like herding a fat cow." was Sweet Pea's reply.

The Gnome/ Stage Manager stuck his head in the door and shouted "Five minutes flowers–five minutes."

Lining up in the wing waiting for their entrance cue, the flowers made their final costume adjustments. Several did exercise movements to be sure they were limber enough for the waltz.

The Dance Mistress said to Wisteria, "No dear, you are number five in the line, not number three. Please take your proper place."

"Oh, silly me." Wisteria giggled and moved to position five.

Not a brain in her head, the Dance Mistress thought, *but she sure can dance!*

The flowers danced their waltz splendidly that evening.

The audience loved it, and them.

33

BLUEBELL AND THE OLD FISHERMAN

This story is one of a series about Bluebell,
a dyslectic faerie

Bluebell is descended from a mortal, Psyche. You may remember that the goddess Venus had placed a curse upon Psyche. Under this curse Psyche was never to find a suitable man for a husband and would spend all her days unmarried and alone.

Bluebell the faerie is unaware that, as a descendent of Psyche, she has inherited this terrible curse. Therefore, like all young faeries, Bluebell goes through life looking for "Mister Right," never realizing the futility of her search because of the ancient curse.

However, as you know, faeries never grow old and never change their appearance. Unfortunately the frustration of looking and looking for a mate, and never finding one, caused a number of changes in Bluebell, and especially to her brain which now-a-days looks like a bowl of oatmeal.

To visualize Bluebell you could think of her as looking like Tinkerbelle of Walt Disney fame. Tinkerbelle, of course, is only a tiny faerie whereas Bluebell is in full human scale. She has long flowing, blond hair, beautiful blue eyes, and a beautiful figure. From time to time, she has difficulty keeping her wings on straight but that does not detract from her beauty.

If you will imagine all of this flowing, faerie-like beauty with the i.q. of a basset hound, you will have an idea of what Bluebell is like today.

Despite her mental difficulties, she has many endearing qualities. She is a truly kind-hearted faerie who wants to do good in the world and be as helpful as she can to human folk. Her intentions are to use her magic faerie powers to make the world a better and happier place for humans and faeries alike ... though admittedly things often go astray for Bluebell.

Take the case of Bluebell and the old fisherman for example. Now this old fisherman was not only old but he was also very poor. He was so old that he barely had the strength to go out in his little boat every day to try to catch some fish. On most days, he could catch only enough for his own dinner. He seldom had any left over to sell in the market place.

The old fisherman's greatest fear was that one day he would not be able fish at all, and then he would be carted off to an old folk's home. That was a place he dreaded with all his heart and so he kept on trying to fish just to keep away from that horrible place.

Bluebell had heard that there were many handsome young fishermen in this town. So, she came to the village to see if one of them might be the mister right she has been looking for.

In her search for a handsome young man one evening Bluebell came across the poor old fisherman. She could see that his meager dinner consisted of just one small fish and a piece of bread.

"Oh dear," she said. "Is that all you have to eat?"

"Yes," replied the old man, "But it is enough to keep me out of the old folks home, so I am content."

My goodness, Bluebell thought to herself. *This will never do. Tomorrow I will watch the old man when he goes out to fish and see what i can do to help him.*

As always, Bluebell had the best, and kindest of intentions, in mind.

The next day Bluebell flew out over the old man's boat and waited to see what would happen. The old fisherman baited his hook and dropped it into the water. Before long, a large fish bit on the hook. But when he tried to pull it into the boat the old man did not have enough strength, and he had to let the fish go.

Ah ha, Bluebell thought. *Now I see the problem. The poor old man can only catch small fish. Well, I can take care of that,* She said to herself.

The incantation for catching fish goes like this: "Abra cadabra, I command a big fish to jump into this boat." But being more than a little bit dyslectic, Bluebell, had trouble remembering the exact words of the incantation. What she actually said was, "Abra cadabra! Now I command a bigger fish to jump into this boat."

Satisfied with herself, and convinced that she had solved the old fisherman's problem, Bluebell flew off to Portugal where she heard there were many handsome young men.

The next day, when the old fisherman went out to fish, as if by a miracle, a large fish jumped into his boat. "This is wonderful," said the old man. "With this large fish I will have a good dinner tonight."

The following day an even larger fish jumped into the old man's boat. "This is a miracle," cried the old man. "Not only will I have a good dinner tonight but there will be enough fish left over for me to sell in the market."

Every day a fish jumped into the old man's boat, and every day the fish got larger and larger and larger. Until one day, a whale tried to jump into the boat. The whale, of course, was so large it sank the old man's boat.

Since the old fisherman was no longer able to fish and support himself, he was soon carted off to the old folk's home, where he spent the rest of his days in misery, and in cursing Bluebell the dyslectic faerie.

34

FEAR OF FLYING

"Did you see what happened?" the Faerie Flying Instructor asked Daffodil.

"Yes, I saw it all, from the beginning to the crash."

"Tell me about it."

"Well, I could see that she was having trouble getting off the ground. She bounced twice before she finally became airborne. Then she didn't seem to be able to gain any altitude, and so she crashed into the trees at the end of the field."

The Flying Instructor sighed. "I don't know what I'm going to do about Bluebell. I am not supposed to teach her how to fly. All Faeries are supposed to know how to fly. It's what we do! My job is just to see that she does it safely and gracefully. We are all supposed to be inspirations for the younger faeries. This is Bluebell's second crash this week."

Bluebell, sitting nearby, and nursing a bruised ankle, overheard this conversation and grew even more depressed. Feeling humiliated, she quietly slipped off to find consolation on the shore of the lake. She was not able to stop her tears, and she sobbed pitifully as she sat by the water's edge.

Presently, a pink flamingo glided down close to the surface of the water, then gracefully flew to the end of the lake and circled back close to where Bluebell sat. Seemingly, with no effort, the flamingo landed in the shallows near the shore. Her landing did not make even a ripple on the water's surface.

"Child, why are you crying so?" the flamingo asked.

"Because I am afraid of flying — that's why I keep crashing. I cannot fly like all the other fairies — I will never earn my magic wand and magic powers! I am a disgrace to my parents," she replied.

"Perhaps I can help you," said the flamingo, "I've been flying for many years now. Some consider me a good teacher."

"Oh yes! Please help me," Bluebell begged.

"Very well, we shall start at once. Now stand up and show me how you move your wings."

Bluebell stood and began flapping her wings frantically.

"Slowly, slowly, dear child," said the flaming. "And when you move your wings upward, angle them like this to save your strength. And when you bring your wings down, angle them like this, to catch the air and raise yourself up."

Bluebell mastered the flapping technique and was beginning to rise up off the ground.

"Now," said the flamingo, "you must know that the most important part of flying occurs inside your mind and it occurs in two stages. The first stage will be your sense of accomplishment and the loss of your fear of flying. The second stage will be a feeling of joy and exhilaration from soaring above the villages and fields."

For the next ten days Bluebell and the flamingo flew together over the village housetops and up into the clouds. What the flamingo said proved to be true, and Bluebell soon became intoxicated with the pure joy of flying.

When Bluebell finally went back to the Faerie Flying School, she amazed the Instructor and all the students by soaring and looping and tumbling high up in the air, smiling all the while as she performed the most difficult aerobatics.

"Do you see what happened?" the Faerie Flying Instructor asked the other students rhetorically. "All of you can do the same if you just lose your fear of flying."

This page left blank so you can write a comment about the preceding story

35

BLUEBELL AND THE SPIDER

"Eeekkkkkkkk!" Bluebell the Fairy shrieked, flapping her wings frantically she flew backward and hovered about four feet from where she had been sitting.

"What is it? What's the matter?" Gardenia asked.

"There's a big spider right next to where I was sitting. Give me a fly swatter or a newspaper so I can kill it."

"Kill it? Now wait just a minute before you do anything as rash as that. Killing is forever, and you might regret it later. Did the spider bite you?"

"No."

"Did it harm you in any way?"

"No."

"Well then, let's just think about this for a minute," said Gardenia, an older and wiser fairy. "That spider might be a Mommy spider. Would you want to deprive her children of their Mother?"

"No," Bluebell answered contritely.

"Maybe that spider is a great philosopher. Would you want to deprive all the other spiders of its wisdom?"

"Of course not," Bluebell answered sheepishly.

"That spider could even be a great poet or artist."

"I never thought of it that way," Bluebell said. "But spiders are creepy-crawly things. They're not like us at all. And they eat flies."

"Humans are not like us. And they eat chickens, so do you want to kill humans too?"

"Hmm."

"I'll tell you what, let's wait until tomorrow. If you still think you want to kill that spider, then you just go ahead and do it. How would that be?" Gardenia asked.

"Okay, I guess that's reasonable. I'll wait until tomorrow."

Dawn came up as a rosy red sunrise. Bluebell flew back to the tree where she had seen the spider the day before. When she arrived, she was astonished to see a huge web that went from the lowest limb of the tree down to the very stump that Bluebell had been sitting on the day before. The spider had spun the web in intricate geometric and circular patterns. It had diagonal strands that added interest and contrast to the circular forms. This marvelous creation was covered with the morning dew. The light from the rising sun refracted through the dewdrops causing the beautiful web to shine with all the colors of the rainbow. The spider web looked like a giant, fantastic, colored crystal.

It was the most beautiful thing Bluebell had ever seen.

Gardenia was right, Bluebell thought, *this spider is a great artist. I was foolish to think about killing it just because it is different than I am.*

Bluebell sat down, reveling at the spider's wonderful creation; and then, after a while, she flew away.

This page left blank so you can write a comment about the preceding story

36

LAMMASTIDE

The wheel of the year has turned once more
And the harvest will soon be upon us.
We have food on our tables,
and the soil is fertile
Nature's bounty, the gift of the earth
gives us reason to be thankful.
Mother of the harvest, with your sickle and basket
Bless me with abundance and plenty
                 Chant recited during the Lammastide festival.

County Kerry lies on the southwestern tip of Ireland. The county contains one of the few mountain ranges in Ireland. The mountains are called Macgillicuddy's Reeks.

In a local pub two strangers strike up a conversation over their pints of Guinness stout.

"So, it's an American you are, then?" The local man asked.

"Yes." Kevin McLaughlin answered.

"And you're leaving America to move here to Ireland?"

"Yes."

"And why would you be doin' such a ting as that?"

"I'm sick of the gun violence, political skullduggery and racial bigotry in America, among other things."

"And you think you'll get away from all that and find peace and harmony here in Ireland?"

"I hope so, yes. But right now I'm looking for a piece of land that I can build a house on."

"That should not be too difficult. These mountains are not very conducive to farming, though there is some in the valleys. If I were you, I'd take the road that goes from Molls Gap to Portmagee. You may find some land along the way."

"Thanks, I'll do just that in the morning."

Two days later Kevin entered a local real estate office

"Are you Mr. Ryan the Real Estate Agent?" he asked

"I am that." Ryan replied.

"I saw your sign on that piece of land about three kilometers outside of town. If the price is right, I might be interested in buying it."

Ten days later Kevin and Mr. Ryan met in the real estate office to close the land purchase.

"Well, there you are then, Mr. McLaughlin. You are now the proud owner of four acres of valley land. And a fine view of the lake as well."

"Yes. All I need now is a contractor to build the house I have in mind for that lovely piece of land."

"You'll not find a contractor, as such, in this remote part of Ireland Mr. McLaughlin. But let me suggest John O'Brien to you. He does most of the building around here— barns and farm sheds, and such as that. He's a fine carpenter."

"Thanks, I'll look him up."

John O'Brien, the carpenter, and Kevin were standing in the middle of Kevin's new piece of land looking at some sketches of a small cottage.

"I know my sketches are rough but I think you get the idea. Can you build it for me, John?"

"Well, it looks simple enough it's a typical Irish stone cottage; just three rooms and two fireplaces. The thatch roof will be a problem, though. There aren't any Thatcher's left in this county. I'd have to bring in a couple of men from up

Limerick way, and they would have to supply the thatch as well. It'll cost ya, but it can be done. But that's not what worries me the most."

"What do you mean? What worries you?"

"It's the faeries."

"The what? Did you say faeries?"

"Yes, I did."

"John, what on earth are you talking about?"

"You've bought a lovely piece of land, and all, but it runs right across a faerie pathway. Let me explain. Look over here to the west. That high hill that you see is called Carrauntoohil. Now look over here to the east. The hill that you see there is called Croach Mhor. Both those hills are faerie hills. They are where the faeries live and keep their gold. Every year during Lammastide they move from one hill to the other, and your land lies right across the pathway the faeries have been using for hundreds of years. No good will come of it if you try to block their path. The little people can move houses and castles if they've a mind to."

"John, you're a grown man. You can't honestly believe such nonsense."

"I'm not saying I do, and I'm not saying I don't. I'm just telling you what people around here believe to be true."

"Well, when does this Lammastide happen?"

"It starts on the first day of August and lasts for the entire month. It's a festival to celebrate the end of summer and the start of harvest time."

"That gives us seven months to build my cottage. Will you do it?"

"All right, Mr. McLaughlin, I can use the money. I'll build your cottage — but no good will come of it, I'm telling ya."

Seven months later Kevin and Mr. O'Brien were standing in front of the new cottage. "It's beautiful John! It's just the way I saw it in my mind's eye. I can't thank you enough. And we beat the calendar. Lammastide doesn't start for two weeks yet."

August first. Kevin McLaughlin shut down his computer and went to bed around 10:30p.m. That night, at about 2:00a.m., strange noises from outside the cottage woke him up. By August fourth the noises had become a combination of shrieks, yells and weird singing. On the night of August ninth, the house was shaken as if by a small earthquake.

The next day, thoroughly frightened and now a believer in faeries, Kevin called John O'Brien back to his house. John came with his father. Kevin described what had been going on since the start of Lammastide and beseeched John for some advice on what to do.

O'Brien was at a loss for creative suggestions. He said he was a carpenter not an expert on faerie lore. At last, his father spoke up. "It's the faeries for sure — and they must be in a rage because your house is blocking their pathway. Now, if there were some way to move your house, or unblock the pathway, I'm sure the faeries would leave you alone. It is known by one and all that faeries mean no harm to humans... Hmmm," he said, "let me take another look at your house."

With that, the old man walked all around the cottage and then inspected the inside. When he came out he said, "I have an idea. If you knock out part of the back wall of the cottage and put in another door, directly opposite the front door, that might open the pathway for the faeries."

"I'll try anything," Kevin said. "Let's get to work, John."

By nightfall the new door, directly opposite the front door, was installed. The three humans sat in the living room of the cottage waiting to see what would happen. At about one o'clock in the morning the sound of music and revelers approaching the cottage was heard. What followed was a parade of faerie folk of all sizes and shapes carrying bags and chests of gold. They paraded in through the front door and out through the back door of the cottage, seemingly for hours. The last of them to pass through the house was a wizened little man wearing a three cornered hat, and pointy-toed shoes. A clay pipe was clamped between his teeth. Just as he was about to leave the cottage he turned and smiled at the three humans. Then he gave them a big wink, jumped two feet in the air, clicked his heels, and skipped out the back door.

37

SAINTS PRESERVE US

As was their custom of a Sunday, James O'Brien and Michael Day went fishing on Lake Killarney. They packed their fishing poles, bait, a bit of lunch, and several cans of Guinness Stout into Michael's small boat and rowed out to the middle of the lake. That particular Sunday the weather was glorious and the fish were biting well enough.

"'Tis hot work," said James, as he opened another can of Guinness.

"So 'tis," agreed Michael, as he finished his third can of the morning.

By mid-afternoon, when the Guinness was gone, both men agreed that they had had enough fishing for the day.

"I'll just try me luck one last time," James said, as he threw his baited hook into the lake. They began a discussion of the Irish rugby games and were not paying much attention to James' fishing pole. Suddenly the reel began to spin madly and howl like a banshee.

"Look to it, look to it," Michael cried. "Sure, it must be a whale!!"

"Whatever 'tis, it fights like a demon. But I'll not give in. Sure, your mint this day." said James, as he struggled to bring the catch up to the side of the boat. "Get ready with the net for I think I've got him now."

Together, the two men fought the mystery catch. Finally they netted it and hauled it into the small boat. To their astonishment, it was a leprechaun.

"Keep the net on him. Don't let him get away," cried Michael. Both men took hold of the leprechaun and held him fast.

It was an evil looking thing, with beady red eyes, long teeth, pointed finger nails and a long beard that came down to its waist.

"All right, all right," said the leprechaun. "There's no need to hold me so tight, tangled up in this net as I am., I've no chance of getting away...I suppose you'll be wanting your three wishes before you set me free."

"Begorra, I've waited all me life for a chance like this, and I'll have me three wishes from ye." Whereupon James and Michael entered into a discussion about what the first wish should be.

"Come on, come on," said the leprechaun. "I don't have all day."

After much discussion the two fishermen came to an agreement about the first wish.

"Me first wish," said James, "is that you turn this entire lake into Guinness stout."

"Done," cried the leprechaun. And so all the waters of lake Killarney were turned into Ireland's favorite drink.

"Ah," said Michael, "tis a fine thing you've done this day. Now let me suggest that before you make your second wish we take this leprechaun back to the shore so we can give proper thought to your second wish."

"A fine idea," agreed James. "You hold onto the leprechaun and I'll row us back to shore."

James took up the oars and started to row, but the boat would not move. Not one inch, whereupon the leprechaun began to laugh diabolically.

"Fool that you are," said the leprechaun. "Don't you know that beer is thicker than water and you cannot row a boat in it?"

"Faith, were stranded here in the middle of the lake," said James. "We'll surely die of starvation out here. What are we to do now?"

The leprechaun laughed.

The two fishermen went into a huddled conversation to decide what the second wish would be. Finally, Michael addressed the leprechaun. "You're a rogue, but not as clever as you think you are. If we cannot row this boat, we will sail it to shore. We've enough coats and oars to make a sail. When we've done that, the second wish will be for a wind to blow us back to shore. And when we get there, we'll still have one wish left as our due."

So Michael and James made a sail for the boat, and James said, "All right now, give us some wind so we can sail to shore."

"Done," cried the leprechaun. Soon a fierce wind began to blow— and blow. Waves began to appear, one after the other, as the wild storm turned the lake into a madly churning sea of Guinness stout. The little boat was tipped and tossed about until finally a great wave of beer came and capsized it throwing James and Michael into the lake.

"Hellp me, help me," Michael cried, "for I can't swim a stroke. and I'm drowning in a lake of Guinness stout. Tis not a bad way to go, but I'm not ready to die yet."

"I'll be no help to ye," shouted James above the roar of the storm, "for I'm no swimmer meself. Saints preserve us but I wish I'd never seen this day."

Instantly, both men found themselves on the shore with no fish, no boat and nothing but water in the lake. And it was still Sunday.

150

"There'll be no fishing next Sunday;" said Michael

And out on the lake they could hear the laughter of the leprechaun.

38

A NICE VINTAGE BUT RATHER FRUITY

"I say we plug her now. She's only a hooker. Even the cops won't care about one more dead hooker." Taurus said.

"Now wait a minute, wait a minute. Let's not rush into this. I mean we don't want to do anything rash, do we? Do we? Once that's done there's no going back," Crabby replied.

"Couldn't you guys just slap her around a bit? I mean that's such a pretty dress. I'd hate to see it all covered with blood. And think of how much the dry cleaning would cost for something like that." Helen chipped in.

They stood quietly for a moment, looking down at the limp body of the unconscious prostitute lying sprawled out on the floor of the back room of the liquor store.

"Jeeze," Crabby said to Taurus. "You really stiffed her with that punch. I thought her head was going to come off."

"What did you expect me to do when she started screaming? She coulda raised the whole neighborhood."

"Well I don't blame her," Helen said. "We thought this was going to be a nice quiet party before we got around to ...well you know what. I even had my hair done."

"It woulda been a nice quiet party if you ladies hadn't raised the price of your services. Neither of us carries that kind of cash around. Breaking into this liquor store was the only way we could come up with some quick cash," Taurus said.

"Okay, okay," Crabby butted in. "I don't think she'll run to the cops just because she panicked when she realized what we were doing. So I don't think we have to kill her. Helen is right. If we just slap her around a bit and warn her of the consequences of going to the cops, she'll keep her mouth shut. Let's wake her up and talk it over. Now how are we going to wake her up?"

"I'll get some cold beer from the cooler and pour it over her," Taurus offered.

"Beer! I knew you didn't have any class as soon as I laid eyes on you," Helen almost shouted. "Gracie is a high-class dame. She deserves champagne. There must be some somewhere around this place."

"Okay, champagne," Taurus grumbled as he ambled off in search of some.

"Help me sit her up," Crabby said.

Together, Helen and Crabby moved the semi-conscious Gracie into a sitting position and leaned her back against a bourbon display case. 'She looks better already," Crabby said.

Taurus returned carrying a case of Armand du Brignac Gold and four Champaign flutes. "This must be good stuff," he said. "Three hundred bucks a bottle."

All three sat on the floor around Gracie. Crabby popped the first cork and Helen, acting as hostess, poured drinks all around. Once revived, Gracie listened to the options Taurus proposed— bump her off or promise to keep her mouth shut. Gracie, a practical girl, agreed not to talk. That called for a toast.

They all agreed the champagne was good stuff and why not just have their little party right there? So one bottle led to another and another and...when Henry Curtis opened the liquor store the next morning, he took his time calling the police.

"No rush," he told the desk sergeant. "These four aren't going anywhere soon. It cost me eighteen hundred dollars for a case of my best champagne, but it will be worth it to see their faces when you revive them."

39

THE HOMECOMING

The year 1936 was not a very good one for the small city of Braunau am Inn (Braunau on the Inn river) in Upper Austria. The worldwide depression had reached Austria, and for a while residents of this small city had to do some belt tightening.

The next year, 1937, was better. Some tourists had begun to return for the winter skiing in the Austrian Alps and many of the shops in the city had come out of the most difficult economic times.

For twelve-year-old Annemarie Schuetz life was good. Just this year, 1938, her father had been given a job in the post office, and her mother had taken a sales position in one of the shops on the old city square.

Most mornings Annemarie awoke with a smile and looked forward to her day at the Catholic school just next to St. Stephens's cathedral. Even though the Schuetz family was part of the small Jewish community in Braunau, there were only six families in the congregation, and Annemarie loved her days with the nuns and all her Catholic friends.

Like all young Austrian girls Annemarie was taught many household skills, such as knitting and cooking, in addition to the usual academic subjects.

Sundays were a special delight for Annemarie, her mother, and her father. Mother and Annemarie got to put on their dirndl dresses with all the hand embroidery and the crisp white blouses. Father always looked splendid in his knee pants and the hat with the wide round brim and a feather stuck in its band.

Dressed as proud Austrians, the Schuetzes would walk through the old town square and on to the park where, when the weather was fine, there would be music, games, street vendors and performers. Of course, on the way home, the family would stop in Herr Stolte's pastry shop where father and mother would have a coffee and the family would share a kaiserschmarenn with raspberry sauce.

Often in the evenings mother and father would sit and talk seriously about the turmoil in Vienna. Annemarie did not understand much of their conversation. But she often heard new words such as Nazis, and something called National Socialism about which she knew nothing.

One day there was even a demonstration on the old town square. Men in brown shirts and leather belts marched around the square with drums beating and flags flying in the breeze. The flags had a strange sort of cross on them. The Braunau police seemed to think these men were actually causing a disturbance, and soon the police broke up their demonstration and chased the men in brown shirts off the square.

The town soon returned to its old idyllic self. The demonstration was quickly forgotten. The only part of the demonstration that Annemarie could remember was the men shouting "Heil Hitler" over and over again. Apparently, Herr Hitler was some sort of hero to the men in the brown shirts, though Annemarie could not tell why.

The Sunday of March 12, 1938, seemed to be a special occasion. The Schuetz family, dressed in their Austrian finery, walked to the old town square. The streets and the square were crowded with many more people than usual, and there was an air of excitement about everything.

The old square looked quite festive because those red-and-white flags, the ones with the crooked cross on them, were hung from many of the buildings. As the Schuetzes reached the square, the crowd surged toward the bridge across the Inn River, the bridge that connected Austria with Bavaria, in Germany.

Annemarie saw a large shiny car with a man standing up in the back coming across the bridge. Many people in the crowd were crying out, "He's coming, he's coming!" She heard the Bürgomeister say "Yes, yes, you see, our native son is returning to the city of his birth."

By this time the big car had reached the town square. German soldiers looking very smart in their gray-green uniforms, and marching with great precision to the drums and bugles, escorted it. The crowds lining the streets were enthusiastically, almost frantically, shouting "Heil Hitler, Heil Hitler!" and raising their arms in the Nazi salute.

Annemarie's mother and father chose not to say the Heil Hitler words but just stood silently as the big car went past.

Many years later, as a survivor of the Holocaust, Annemarie could still hear the drums and see the flags that marked Adolph Hitler's homecoming and started the chain of events that took her parents, and changed her life, and the world, forever.

40

CANDY-APPLE RED

Inmate number No.86550 worked his way across the prison yard, found the man he was looking for, inmate —No.32749— and handed him a wad of cash.

"Conceal this with the rest of the money. By the way, how's the stash doing? Are we going to make the total?"

"Not to worry," No.32749 replied. "We'll make it."

It had taken eighteen months for the money to accumulate, but that had not been the hardest part of the project. First there had been the work of the organizing committee which had come up with the idea. Then the Legal Committee, which had used the prison's extensive law library to see if the project was legal. It was. Next came the What-Should-It-Be Committee. Theirs had been the most contentious task. It took many arguments and several fistfights to arrive at a decision.

Once the legal and the what-it-should-be issues were settled, the whole project had to be organized so that the money could be raised in secret. "Dues" had to be collected from each of the sixteen hundred inmates on a regular basis; an accountant had to be selected (though there were several of these among the inmate population, the most trustworthy had to be chosen); and, of course, a "banker" who would actually hold the money. Inmate No.32749 was the obvious choice for this, since he was a lifer without possibility of parole. Also, as the oldest and longest resident of the prison, he had free rein to all the buildings and therefore the greatest opportunity to find a hiding place for the money.

The original organizing committee had done well to start the project eighteen months earlier. There was a known end date for the project, August 25, 2015, and a lot of work to be done if it was to succeed.

Secrecy was paramount, although, an outside contact person had to be chosen in order to carry out the project. Each corrections officer was carefully screened for the job, and, unbeknown to them, vetted by another committee of inmates. Officer Upton was finally given the nod and in a series of private conversations, the project was revealed to him. To everyone's relief, he not only agreed to act as the outside contact for the prisoners, he declared his personal interest in making the project a success. From time to time he made cash contributions to the project.

Over the course of the eighteen months, prisoners were transferred to this institution from other jails around the country. All of the transferees had heard of the project through the mysterious prison "grapevine". At first, some of them had to be convinced to pay their "dues". But after three or four months, most of them donated willingly to the project. *Greenies*, the new inmates who came to the prison directly from the courts or local county jails, were easily intimidated by their new surroundings, and the "sincerity" of the regular inmates, into supporting the project.

As August 25 approached, a new crisis arose — what color should "it" be? Feelings and passions ran high. One group of inmates insisted on black, as the most dignified color. Another group wanted a bright, celebratory yellow color. Some even rooted for lemon yellow. In the end, the Organizing Committee had to hold a plebiscite on the color issue. When the final votes were tallied, candy-apple red was the winning choice. When word of the results spread throughout the prison yard, inmates could be heard grinning and saying, "Yeah, candy-apple red. That's great." Even the color-black contingent had to give in with a smile and said, "Yeah, candy-apple red will do it."

Finally, the big day arrived. It started like every other day, with all the normal prison routines. There was, however, an air of electricity everywhere, and the excitement was palpable. Lunch for the prisoners was from 11:30 a.m. to 12:45 p.m.. The dining hall was filled with smiles, even a few hugs, and many "Hey, we did its." By 12:55 p.m. the dining hall was empty, and all sixteen hundred inmates were in the prison yard. At precisely 1:15 p.m. all the prisoners sat down on the prison yard's dirt floor. Slowly they began to chant "Warden, warden, warden." The corrections officers grew tense and, following their training protocol, surrounded the sitting prisoners.

"Warden, warden, warden," the prisoners continued to chant.

Captain O'Conner, chief of the corrections officers, stood before the sitting inmates and shouted, "Okay, okay, I don't know what this is all about, but the warden is on his way down here."

It took Warden Miller about five minutes to get from his office to the entrance to the prison yard. As soon as he arrived, the prisoners broke into a fragmented version of "Happy Birthday to You". After two verses, the singing stopped. Inmate No. 33658, the Chairman of the Organizing Committee, stood up and walked over to Warden Miller. In the shortest presentation speech ever made he said, "From all of us to you, the best damn warden in the whole damn prison system." With that, he handed the warden the keys to a brand new, candy-apple-red, Toyota convertible.

41

BACK TO SCHOOL

Oh, Dear Mother of God, I'm going to die. I just know I'm going to die. June 6, 1944. The second invasion wave approached Omaha Beach. *I can see bodies all over the beach. I just know I'm going to die. Why is he lowering the ramp this far from the beach? The water must be four feet deep this far out.*

"This is it," the First Lieutenant said. "Everyone out and hit the beach."

Holding his rifle above his head, he waded in the waist-deep water trying to follow the Lieutenant. Bam! It felt like someone had hit his left forearm with a baseball bat. There was blood and pain, lots of pain. Fortunately, the company medic was just ten feet behind him.

Sheltering behind a disabled jeep the medic loaded his wound with sulfur powder and applied a field dressing. "That's it for you, pal. Both the radius and ulna bones are smashed. Your war is over," the medic said.

It took three days to get him out to a hospital ship and another ten days to get him back to England.

The medic was right. His war was over, and it left him with a left arm that was two inches shorter than his right arm. The army discharged him in November 1945.

Now what am I going to do? Sure, I finished high school before I joined the army but I have no skills, no training in anything. I wonder if this thing called the G.I. Bill can get me started on something. I've always wanted to be an engineer, and I'm pretty good at math.

His graduation from the mechanical engineering program at Georgia Tech occurred in June 1950. The postwar automobile industry was booming then so he went off to Detroit.

One day in July 1955, his boss, the chief design engineer, called him into his office.

"I don't see any way around it," said the chief. "These Trafficators have been used in Europe for almost ten years now. Our competition is already offering them on their high-end models so we are playing catch-up here. Considering the handicap you have with your left arm, I'm putting you in charge of a small team to work on them for our '58 model. I know you can do it."

At the 1958, Chicago Auto Show a scantily dressed young woman pulled the cover off the new model as the emcee extolled the virtues and features of the shiny new sedan. Toward the end of his fifteen-minute spiel he said, "And as an added safety feature on this year's models they will all be equipped with flashing lights, front and rear, to show other drivers your intention to turn. We call it the *Turn Signal.* Never again will you have to stick your left arm out the window to give those old-fashioned hand signals."

This page left blank so you can write a comment about the preceding story

42

MEDIUM STARCH

You would never suspect Vincent "Vinnie" Scaduto of being an evil person just by looking at him. He spent years developing the look of a well-to-do, middle class businessman. He kept an active charge account at the San Francisco Brooks Brothers store on Union Square. Everything he wore came from that store. "Shirts and ties make the image," Vinnie always said. His ties were BB's Small Medallion Print ($98.50), and his shirts were BB's Traditional Fit Button-down Collar Dress Shirts ($95.00). No exceptions.

To protect his substantial investment in BB shirts, Vinnie searched all over San Francisco for a laundry that would appreciate his fastidiousness. Local dry cleaners and large commercial laundries often would ruin them with strong bleaches and harsh machines. No, a hand laundry was what he wanted. He finally found a Chinese hand laundry at 21 Clay Street in Chinatown.

San Francisco's Chinatown is home to about seventy thousand inhabitants, most of whom speak the Cantonese dialect and a smattering of broken English. Approximately one percent of the residents are illegal immigrants who manage to bury themselves in the hurly-burly of Chinatown. Living quietly and staying out of trouble had kept most of them out of the clutches of the U.S. Immigration and Naturalization Service (INS).

At the laundry, Vinnie found Bojing Ma, the owner, and his attractive wife, Lanying. Together they worked the laundry twelve to sixteen hours a day, lived in the back room, bothered no one, and managed to evade the INS for six years.

Vinnie's first visit to their shop lasted thirty minutes while he quizzed Bojing on how he laundered shirts and how they would be hand-pressed by Lanying. It took a while for Vinnie to get the idea of medium starch across to Bojing, but it finally seemed to sink in. Vinnie's next concern was how to ensure that his shirts would not get mixed up with someone else's. Finally, Bojing said, "I mark, I mark." then he showed Vinnie how he would mark the inside of the bottom hem with Chinese characters to distinguish Vinnie's shirts from all others.

Satisfied that he had found the right place, Vinnie left two shirts as a trial run. When he picked them up a few days later he was pleased with the work and decided that his shirts had found their second home. For the next six months things went well. Then, one day while Bojing was out of the shop, Vinnie made his move on Lanying.

He hadn't gotten much further than making a few improper gestures to Lanying and showing her several hundred dollar bills when Bojing returned. The atmosphere in the shop was tense, and Linyang looked frightened. Vinnie put his shirts on the counter and left.

For several hours that evening Bojing and Linyang discussed this new and dangerous situation. They had the feeling that, somehow, Vinnie was a dangerous person. At the very least, he could turn them over to the INS if they confronted him directly. In the end, they decided to assume a stoic attitude toward him and see what developed.

A crisis did develop two weeks later, when Vinnie brought in five shirts, one of which had blood stains right at the belt line. "Can you fix it?" Vinnie asked.

"I fix, I fix, no problem," Bojing replied.

Patty Wong was a part-time prostitute. Part-time in that she only had three carefully selected clients, who visited her on a highly structured schedule to ensure that none of them ever visited at the same time. However, the best-laid plans of mice and prostitutes often go astray, as we know, and Vinnie arrived one evening just as client number two was leaving. He spent the night with Patty, and the next morning, after getting dressed, he beat her to a bloody pulp. He left an extra one hundred dollars on her dresser.

The paramedics took Patty to the Bay Area Chinese Hospital where she had several weeks to recover and consider her relationship with Vinnie. When she finally came to a decision, she telephoned detective Frank Liu at the Chinatown Division of the San Francisco PD. Frank paid her a visit at the hospital.

"Listen Frank," Patty said. "You've been good to me a couple of times in the past, so I think I owe you. I see from the *Chronical* you're working on that series of U Frisco co-ed murders, aren't you?"

"Yeah. Everyone knows that. Even the *Chinatown News* is covering the story. So whaddya got for me?"

"Well, this may be a long shot, but I think you should pay a visit to the Chinese Hand Laundry at 21 Clay Street."

"Why? What have you heard?"

"I haven't heard anything. It's what I saw. You just go visit that laundry, okay?"

"If you say so. If this turns out to be anything, we'll be even. Thanks Patty."

Frank's visit with Bojing and Lanying only lasted an hour. That's all it took for Frank and Bojing to make a deal. One bloody shirt for a promise not to involve the INS, and $95.00 to reimburse Bojing for one BB Traditional-fit, Button-down Collar Shirt.

DNA tests tied Vinnie to one of the murdered co-eds, and the rest is history.

The next time Frank saw Patty he couldn't refrain from asking her what it was she saw that led her to point him to the hand laundry.

"That was easy," Patty said. "There were Chinese characters on the bottom of Vinnie's shirt that read, 'Bad man. Murderer'."

"Hmmm. Very clever, these Chinese." Frank murmured.

43

CHINESE COOKING–101

"Chicken or Pork?" Jean asked.

"We're using chicken tonight." Lucy Cheng, the instructor, answered, "I was afraid some people in the class might not eat pork so I decided on chicken."

"Where does the 'hot' in hot and sour soup come from?" Helen wanted to know.

"Some of it comes from vinegar and some of it comes from chili peppers."

"Hey, Chili peppers," Enrique chimed in, "just like we Mexicans use in Chili Rellenos. I can dig that."

"Okay, that's enough questions for now," Lucy Cheng answered, "It's time to start cooking. You'll find all the ingredients you need at your cooking stations, so let's get to it."

The class broke into groups of three and went to their cooking stations. Jean's group consisted of Jean, Enrique the young Mexican man, and an older woman named Henrietta.

"I'll do the dicing and chopping," Enrique said, "We Mexicans are good with the knife," he added with an innocent smile.

"Okay, I'll take care of the tofu, the bean sprouts, the lilly buds, and the wood ears," Jean offered.

"That leaves the seasoning mix, the eggs, and the cornstarch for me." Henrietta said. "Now let me see, here's the Soy sauce, the mushroom powder, white pepper, vinegar, and sugar. Okay, I guess I've got it all."

The students set about their work. Enrique noticed that Henrietta was eyeing him suspiciously as he sliced the chicken breast. "What's the matter Tia Henrietta," He asked sarcastically, "Don't you trust me?"

"I just want to be sure you're doing it correctly. Chinese cooking is very precise, unlike Mexican cooking where you can just throw things together."

"Listen, old Tia, I've been cooking with my abuela for years. She is a great cook and she's taught me everything I know. So don't worry about a thing. I know what I'm doing, okay?"

Henrietta turned away with a snort and murmured "Old tia!! Smart ass kid."

Eventually, all the ingredients were ready and the pot of water was boiling. According to Lucy Cheng's recipe the ingredients had to be added in a particular order, and each one, at just the right time. Enrique stood over the pot; spoon in hand, ready to stir as Jean added each ingredient. In due course, it was time to add the mixture of cornstarch and water. While Jean added it, Enrique stirred. Henrietta was pouring over the recipe, contemplating the next item when she happened to glance over at Enrique. Almost apoplectic, she let out a scream.

"EEEeeeek! What are you doing? Are you out of your mind!!"

Jean and Enrique froze. "What? What's wrong? All I'm doing is stirring the soup." Enrique said.

"Yes, but look at how you're stirring it," an exasperated Henrietta said, "You're doing it all wrong."

"No, this is exactly how my Abuela taught me to stir soup. You put the spoon into the pot until it touches the bottom and then you stir in a figure-eight pattern. That way you mix everything evenly."

"That may work for Pozole, but your Abuela has just ruined our soup."

"Leave my abuela out of this," Enrique growled.

"Here, look at the recipe," Henrietta said, "It explicitly says to stir IN ONE DIRECTION ONLY! You've ruined our soup. Look at it; it's turned a deathly gray color."

Ever the peacemaker, Jean spoke up, "Well, it's done now. We might as well finish it and see what happens. What's the next ingredient?"

"The eggs," Henrietta replied, "and they must be stirred in one direction only."

"Okay, okay, I get it," from Enrique

An air of hostility and tension hung over the team as they completed the recipe. When the soup was done, spoons and bowls were produced and the students gingerly tasted their concoction.

Silence.

More silence.

"Hmmm," from Jean.

"Hey, this is pretty good!" from Enrique

"This is downright delicious. Amazing!" was Henrietta's judgment.

"Yes, but look at it. It doesn't look like any hot and sour soup I've ever seen."

"Don't worry; in Mexico, we have a simple solution for a cooking disaster such as this."

"Oh, and what might that be?" Henrietta asked.

"It's simple; we just change the name of the dish," Enrique said with a sly grin. "So let's just call this Nouveau Hot and Sour Soup."

By this time Lucy Cheng was going from team to team to view their accomplishments. When she got to Jean's team she looked into the pot, gasped, pointed a finger at the pot and demanded to know "What is this?"

"Nouveau Hot and Sour Soup!" The three students responded in one voice.

Lucy Cheng gave a sigh, rolled her eyes, threw up her arms and simply walked away.

174

44

MR. MINSKY'S PAWN SHOP

Ahh Brooklyn. If it were a separate city. and not one of New York's boroughs, it would be the third most populous city in the United States. Its population of 2.5 million souls is almost evenly divided between Jewish, Irish, Italian, Russian, Polish, Hispanic and African Americans. A pawnshop owner, Mr. Minsky, lived in a neighborhood called Ocean Parkway, a mostly Jewish section, just north of Coney Island.

Every morning after his ritual visit to the synagogue, Mr. Minsky would board the Ocean Parkway bus at Avenue L and ride it south to Avenue U, where his Pawn Shop was located. The ride from Avenue L to Avenue U was like going from one country into another. Avenue U is in Gravesend, a mostly, low-income, ethnically mixed section of Brooklyn

Gravesend stands on a razor-thin line between lower middle class and poverty. It is exactly the kind of neighborhood than needs a pawnshop, and Minsky's Pawn Shop had been an institution in Gravesend for twenty-seven years.

Mr. Minsky was both loved and hated in the neighborhood. For some it was, "Thank God for Mr. Minsky, he gave me ten dollars for an old toaster just because he knew my Social Security check would not come in the mail for another six days." For others, it was, "Damn that miserly Jew. He could see I needed a fix and he would only give me three dollars for a fifty-dollar watch. Not even enough to buy a single hit."

Jake Connerly was a small-time crook, a drunk, and a wife beater with an explosive temper. If he made it home in his half-drunk condition, he would take out his rage against the world on his wife, Joan. The only reason Joan stayed with Jake was because she was terrified of him. The law finally caught up with Jake, and he was sentenced to two years as a guest of the State of New York at its prison in Ossining.

Joan was attractive, if somewhat plain-looking. She always dressed very simply, but she carried herself with an air of distinction and grace. The more one contemplated the soft-spoken, well-mannered Joan, the more attractive she became.

When Jake was released from prison at the end of his two-year sentence, he was given a check for forty dollars as payment for his work in the prison laundry. That was all the money he and Joan had to their name. By the time he got home, he had spent half of it at a local bar and got just drunk enough to give Joan a black eye.

The next day, while trying to figure out how to get more money, Jake noticed the sparkly ring Joan was wearing.

"Where did you get that?"

"I picked it up at a second-hand store. It's just paste, but I thought it was pretty."

"It sure looks real to me. But what do I know about fake jewelry. I wonder how much it's worth."

"Not much. I only paid three dollars for it."

"I wonder if we can fool the pawn shop owner with it. Come on, we're going to Mr. Minsky's.

Joan protested, saying that she had become fond of the ring and wanted to keep it. That got her a swift slap in the face and an order to, "Keep quiet unless she wanted to have a second black eye."

Mr. Minsky knew Jake and Joan and their history. He also saw the condition of Joan's eye. Then when he put his jeweler's glass to the ring he was amazed to see that it was several carats and nicely cut. *Four to six thousand dollars* he said to himself. *I wonder where she got it?* As he took the glass from his eye and was about to tell them the good news, he glanced at Joan. She was trembling, and fine beads of perspiration had formed on her forehead and upper lip. He understood at once.

"Mrs. Connerly, you were very lucky at that store. This is a nice cubic zirconium fake diamond. I can give you fifty dollars for it."

"Done," cried Jake. They took the money and left the shop.

As they left the shop Mr Minsky thought to himself *I must remember never to leave an attractive woman alone if I am ever sent to prison.*

Two weeks later, Joan came into the shop, thanked Mr. Minsky for his understanding, gave him back his fifty dollars, and redeemed her ring.

45

SPOOKY JENKOWSKI

On Manhattan's Upper West Side there is an area bound by Central Park West, Riverside Drive, 72nd Street and 110th Street. This area of 152 city blocks contains eight houses of prostitution. Spooky Jenkowski was a regular customer at all of them.

When Spooky was not selling hot ice down in the diamond district, he could be found in one of these eight "beauty parlors." What was unusual about Spooky's behavior was that most of his visits were not with one of the "Ladies" but just to hang out in the establishment.

He knew all of the ladies and was civil and polite, to them, yet, there was something terrifying about him. He seemed to be looking for something, or someone, with an air of sinister determination. That's how he earned the name Spooky.

If there was a bar in the establishment, Spooky would often just spend the night sitting at the bar, sipping a drink and watching.

His most often visited beauty parlor was Mitzie Klein's. It was a notch higher than other similar establishments. She had purchased the house next door, and made a pleasant patio and bar area from the yards at the rear of both houses. When the weather was fine, some of the Johns and ladies would sit out there for a quiet drink and a chat.

Spooky would take a table in a corner of the patio, where he could sit and observe the men who came to visit.

Eventually, Mitzie struck up a kind of arms-length friendship with Spooky and when business was slow, she would often sit and chat with him at "his table."

Finally, when she could stand the mystery no longer, she dared to ask him what, or who, he was looking for.

"A man with a scar across his forehead," Spooky told her.

"Why?" she asked.

"It's a complicated story, but it goes like this. Some years ago, he and I were competing for a woman. We came to blows. I managed to put that scar across his face but in the end, he was the lucky one. I mean to have my revenge. I know about Scarface's passion for prostitutes, and I am sure he will show up at one of these beauty parlors eventually, and when he does, I intend to kill him."

Mitzie did not press the conversation further, She walked away and left Spooky to his own seething, brooding, hatred for the man with the scar.

One hot summer August night Scar face did show at Mitzie's. Knives flashed...when the fight was over, Scar face lay dead on the patio. Spooky was dying from multiple knife wounds.

Mitzie took the dying man in her arms and asked, "Are you satisfied now that you've killed the man who stole your girl?"

Barely able to speak, Spooky gasped out his last words, "You don't understand. I won the girl... she ruined my life. I swore I would kill him for what she did to me."

46

DAKOTA RED

In 1827, in Philadelphia, Mrs. Mary O'Conner gave birth to fraternal twins. She named them Constance and John.

Their father, Andrew O'Conner, was a wealthy shipping magnate who doted on the twins and raised them into a comfortable lifestyle. The children were educated in the best schools and were taught solid Christian principles of fairness and justice.

By 1848 Constance had grown into a lovely young woman who found her life's calling in the ballet. She pursued her studies at the Philadelphia Conservatory.

Her brother John had grown to be a likeable but restless youth who showed no interest in taking over his father's shipping business. Life was a great adventure to John, and with so many choices available to him, he had trouble deciding what to do with himself.

When gold was discovered in California in 1848, John knew he had to go west to the goldfields for the adventure of it and to make his fortune independent of his father. He set sail from Philadelphia, sailed around Cape Horn, and after a four month journey, arrived in San Francisco. He followed the other forty-niners and staked his claim along the American River, which was the epicenter of the gold fields. In the summer of 1849 he struck gold, and his claim began to return a huge profit.

The claim next to John's was being worked by a ruffian and gambler who went by the name of Dakota Red. Rumor had it that he had killed a man in his home state of North Dakota.

Dakota Red's claim was a dry hole that gave him nothing but hard work and no gold.

In a classic claim-jumping scheme Dakota Red fabricated a dispute over the boundary line between his claim and young John's. They argued, and in the gunfight that ensued, Dakota Red shot John dead. When the news of John's death reached Philadelphia, his family was devastated. Constance grieved for many months over her twin brother's murder.

Following the gunfight Dakota Red took over John's claim. Red worked the claim for a year, reaped a large fortune in gold, then sold the claim off to another miner and retired to the notorious Barbary Coast at the south end of San Francisco.

Dakota Red soon became a person of ill repute amid the rough and tumble life of the Barbary Coast. Despite his unsavory character, Dakota Red proved an astute businessman and began to develop a number of profitable enterprises. In the natural scheme of things along the Barbary Coast, he soon developed a fierce business rivalry with a man named Jack Lane.

Dakota Red and Jack Lane were not just business rivals: they were also competing for the favors of a dance-hall woman called Bad Betty.

Bad Betty seemed to thrive on the rivalry between Dakota Red and Jack Lane and, being wise to the ways of the Barbary Coast, she managed to coax lavish gifts out of both men. When Dakota Red gave her a fine evening gown, Jack Lane topped that with a diamond bracelet. When Dakota gave her a horse and carriage, Jack Lane countered with a suite at the finest hotel on the Coast.

The rivalry between the two men came to a head one Saturday night, in a place called Shanghai Lil's Saloon and Pleasure House. We need not go into the details of what went on upstairs at the Pleasure house. Suffice it to say that the "girls" upstairs were as busy as the bartenders downstairs.

On this particular evening Bad Betty danced first with one man and then with the other, and so it went all evening long. As the liquor flowed, tempers rose and insults flew back and forth between the rivals. It was clear to everyone that blood would be shed that night.

Shanghai Lil, dressed in a long Chinese gown with a slit up one side, her hair in a bun with chopsticks sticking out of it, and wearing a .44 caliber pistol on her hip, knew that she could not afford to have a bloody confrontation in her saloon and pleasure house. Sensing the rising danger, she grabbed one of her waiters and said, "You go find The Judge. Bring him here. Quick, quick!"

Now, of course, The Judge was not a judge at all. What he was, was an elderly gentleman from an old Virginia family who just looked like a judge. He wore a frock coat, a white shirt and a string tie, and comported himself with the manners of a southern gentleman. In years past he had adjudicated several disputes on the Coast. Everyone agreed that his judgments had been wise and fair. That was how he became the unofficial "judge" of the Barbary Coast.

When The Judge was brought into the saloon Shanghai Lil explained the situation to him, he agreed to try to settle the dispute. He soon had the dance floor cleared and set up as a mock courtroom. Dakota Red and Jack Lane sat about ten feet apart, facing each other. The Judge took his place at a table between them. By this time all other activity in the saloon had stopped, and the patrons gathered around the "courtroom" to watch the proceedings. Some of the "girls" from upstairs even came down to watch the fun.

After listening to statements for Dakota Red and Jack Lane, The Judge pondered for a few moments and then announced his decision.

"The only honorable way to settle a dispute between two gentlemen, such as we have here, is with an old-fashioned duel, which, I decree, will take place at dawn tomorrow. "Furthermore," he said, "there is a proviso that goes with this judgment. The proviso is that since Bad Betty here is the cause, prima fascia and de facto, of this dispute she must agree to marry the survivor of said duel."

Flattered by all the attention, and being somewhat liquored up herself, Bad Betty agreed to The Judge's proviso. The saloon crowd cheered The Judge's verdict, and prepared to witness the excitement of the shoot-out.

At dawn the next morning, at the agreed-upon place, Dakota Red, Jack Lane, their seconds, The Judge, a doctor, and several hundred saloon patrons gathered for the spectacle.

Of course, Bad Betty was in the crowd, her face grotesquely covered with makeup. She was wearing her finest gown and a big summer hats such as would be worn at a garden party. She even carried a small pink parasol, just like society ladies do. She passed through the crowd smiling to this one and nodding to that one, as if she were Queen Victoria visiting the colonies. The dance-hall girl was basking in the glory of two prominent businessmen fighting a duel to the death for her hand in marriage.

The two opponents stood back to back, their pistols at the ready. The crowd became still with anticipation. The Judge counted off ten paces: "1, 2, 3, 4, 5, 6, 7, 8, 9, 10." Both men turned and prepared to fire. At that, very instant Bad Betty cried out from the crowd, "Oh Dakota, my love," and fainted to the ground. Upon hearing her shout, Dakota Red turned to look in her direction. That was just enough of a pause for Jack Lane to take aim and shoot Dakota Red through the heart.

The next day as Jack Lane was off making preparing for his elaborate wedding to Bad Betty; she quietly slipped out of her hotel and boarded a stage-coach to Los Angeles, where one of her father's ships was waiting to take her home to Philadelphia.

47

GIDDYAP JOHNSON

"Basta, enough!" Benny the Tailor cried as he threw a copy of the *Daily Racing Form* on the table. "I can't make no sense outta dese picks in today's races. One handicapper says 'Cando is the horse to go with', an dis udda guy says 'Catzanova is a sure ting at seven ta five', an' somebody else says 'Green Dude could win if the track is muddy' A person couldn't even make a decent living wid dat kinda advice."

"I know, I know," chimed in Bam Bam De Luca. "I fell into a hunnert clams, and I can't find no horse I like either. I don't know what dis country is comin' to when a guy can't pick up some easy scratch at da track no more."

"Ya see, ya see, dat's just what I been telling youse guys," Jerry Johnson said. "It's like this guy Karl Marx sez, 'Ya gotta own da means of production.' For years now we been bettin' on the end result of races. Da way to make a killin' is ya gotta own da horse, 'cause da horse is da means of production. Dat's where da real dough is. So dat's why I am gonna buy a race horse."

"Whaaat!" sez Benny the tailor.

"You must be crazy," Bam Bam de Luca observes. "Youse don't know nothin' about horses."

"What's to know?" Jerry answered. "All ya gotta do is get on 'em and say giddyap and if da horse is fast he wins and youse take da money to the bank."

"Yeah but what about training 'em, and feeding 'em, and all dat stuff?"

"I don't have to worry about dat stuff. The guy I'm buyin' dis horse from knows all about dat, an' he's gonna stay on as my trainer."

"Ownin' a horse costs a lot of money. Where'd you get dat kinda dough?"

"Let's just say I got a midnight loan from a Chase Bank branch when I made dat trip to Cincinnati. So now, like Marx says, I'm gonna own da means of production. As for youse guys, if youse can't make up your minds about today's races, maybe it's time to go see Moe the Jew."

Moe the Jew is an honored, highly respected, and unique institution on the street. To begin with, he is an old-fashioned, dapper-looking guy who, in this day and age, still wears spats and a Homburg hat. He is a handicapper who makes his living off the horses, or to put it more correctly, he makes his living off guys who play the horses.

In all his seventy-odd years Moe the Jew has never placed a bet on a horse, but he has studied horses for most of those seventy years. Moe can tell you all the statistics on every horse that has run a race for the past ten years. He knows who their parents were, how much every jockey weighs, when the horse was last seen by a vet, and why. Moe can probably tell you what every horse had for breakfast today.

So when horse players get stuck and can't figure out which horse to bet on, they go to Moe for his picks of the day. Now, he's is not always right ... but he is right much more often than he is wrong.

On the street the unwritten rule is that if Moe the Jew picks a winner for you, he gets ten percent of the winnings. This is how Moe, and his friend Nuch, make their living. Not that Nuch is a handicapper, far from it. His name comes from the Yiddish word *nuchshlepper*, which, loosely translated, means "hanger-on". He is not very bright. Speculation on the street is that he has the I.Q. of a basset hound, which makes him the perfect gofer and companion for Moe. Wherever Moe goes, Nuch follows.

Over the years every one of the hundred or so serious horse players on the street has gone to Moe. In the end they have all made money off his tips. Their aggregate winnings probably come close to seven figures.

Jerry Johnson bought his racehorse. He named it "Wiseguy". In his first three races, Wiseguy finished in the middle of the pack and did not earn any money. The citizens of the street watched and waited for Wiseguy to start winning. They waited, and waited, and waited. Jerry Johnson took a lot of ribbing from one and all. A current joke on the street was to walk past Jerry and say, "Giddyap, giddyap." By the end of the second racing season, Jerry was simply known as "Giddyap Johnson".

One day, when things on the street were very quiet, a bunch of the guys were hanging around Little Augie Martorano's office, aka the back room of the Villa Napoli Restaurant aka the headquarters of the Martorano Mafia Family. In walks Nuch for his afternoon plate of veal scaloppini. Nuch is looking very sad, indeed. When asked, "What's up," he replied, "It's Moe the Jew. He's had a stroke. He's an old man, ya know."

This is heavy news, and the word quickly spreads around the street of the old man's misfortune. The word gets out that Moe is in a nursing home called The Peaceful Palace. Nuch, of course, visits him every day, and then reports to all interested parties on Moe's condition. It turns out that the Peaceful Palace is a very expensive place, and Nuch does not know how much longer Moe can stay there. The looming alternative is the charity ward at the county hospital. This is very distressing news to Little Augie who, like everyone else, has benefited from Moe's advice over the years. So Little Augie calls for a meeting for one and all to come and talk about Moe's situation.

The room was filled with maybe ninety or a hundred people. A number of ideas were tossed out and discussed but none really caught on. Finally, Giddyap Johnson stood up and said as follows, "Youse all know I have dis horse named Wiseguy, who is not doing so good at the track. It is also true dat dis horse is costing me an arm and a leg to maintain, and I would not mind gettin' out from under him. Now, I know a guy who can mix up a cocktail that would make Wiseguy a sure winner in the third race at Belmont Park next Thursday. With his record, the odds against Wiseguy will be around thirteen to one. Now, if everyone in this room was to bet on Wiseguy ...."

The following Friday Nuch deposited a very very large check with the Peaceful Palace, thereby guaranteeing Moe the Jew a comfortable future for many years to come.

Wiseguy died of a heart attack two days later and Giddyap Johnson became a hero all up and down the street and around and about.

48

THE NOT-SO-COLD COLD WAR

The Cold War between the US. and the Soviet Union (USSR) lasted from 1946, which was the end World War II, to 1991, when the Council of Republics of the Supreme Soviet of the USSR recognized the dissolution of the Soviet Union.

Starting in 1970, there were several periods of détente when there was a slight thawing of the hostilities between the two nations. As, for example, in 1972, when the American Bobby Fischer played and defeated the USSR's Boris Spassky to become the world chess champion. That was also the year the Canadian and USSR hockey teams played against each other.

In 1973 the Paris Peace Accords were signed, officially ending the US. involvement in Viet Nam. That was also the year of the first U.S.—USSR joint space program involving the Apollo and the Soyuz space vehicles. Officially, however, the two countries continued to eye each other suspiciously, continued their spy programs, and kept their nuclear weapons at the ready.

The year 1991 was still a long way off.

Whenever these periods of détente occurred, and both sides agreed to "play nice," there would be a sudden spate of nonpolitical, cultural exchanges.

The Bolshoi Ballet would perform in New York, and we in turn would send delegations from nonpolitical professional fields to Moscow.

Architecture fell into the category of a "nonpolitical profession." From 1968 to 1977 Tony Damien was the director of research programs for the American Institute of Architects

(AIA). His office was just a block away from the Washington DC headquarters of the State Department which made it convenient for State to reach across the street and invite him to make the trip to Moscow in 1972 and again in 1974.

His first trip to Moscow became a surprising display of Soviet decadence.

He and two other US. representatives were billeted in a nice hotel just a block from Red Square. The rooms were simple but operating—room clean, and the food was more than acceptable. The representatives were later informed by their hosts at the American Embassy that this was the official KGB hotel. They were asked not to say nasty things while in their rooms so as not to offend the ears of the KGB folks monitoring their conversations.

As guests of the Soviet Union they had a car and a driver, also from the KGB, to take them to their meetings with their Soviet counterparts, to the mandatory tours of housing factories, and to the god awful — but Soviet pride and joy — thirteen—story, housing developments that surrounded Moscow. The KGB driver had no qualms or difficulty in walking unannounced into any apartment in these concrete monstrosities that they wanted to see.

It is useful to remember that these were the days when Muscovites stood in lines for hours for bread and anything else that stores had to sell. Ownership of a car, even the comical Lada, was a wish to be dreamed of by most Russians.

That first trip to Moscow lasted eight days from Sunday to Sunday.

Monday to Friday were days for "exchanging practical information" and for field trips with Russian architects and builders.

The Saturday before their return to the US. was a free day in Moscow. Tony informed the cultural attaché at the American Embassy that he would like to visit some of the splendid churches on Red Square and around Moscow, and that he had an interest in Russian antiques.

The attaché said that the wife of one of the embassy's staff was particularly knowledgeable about these things; he would see if he could arrange for her to escort Tony around the city. She later turned out to be not married at all but part of the Embassy's resident CIA contingent Escorting Tony was a way to ensure that he was not defecting to the USSR or having secret meetings with the KGB.

She met him at his hotel. Since they were not far from Red Square, they agreed to make the day a walking tour. They had a lovely sightseeing and shopping tour. Around lunchtime they found themselves in an older neighborhood not far from the back side of the Kremlin.

On a whim they decided to have lunch at a local restaurant The one they chose had fifteen or twenty tables, most of which were filled with working class people having lunch. As was the local custom Tony and his guide were seated at a table with two other people. Their tablemates, who did not seem to be together, were a middle aged woman and a man in a military uniform replete with many ribbons on his chest. A waitress handed them menus and indicated she would return for their order.

Of course, the menu was in Russian, and neither Tony nor his escort could understand a word of it. This became clear to their tablemates who exchanged glances and smiles at their obvious quandary. The man in the uniform watched them struggle with the menu for several minutes and then he reached across the table and took possession of Tony's menu.

He indicated by gestures that he was going to order lunch for them.

He and the elderly woman then entered into a laughing conversation, apparently discussing what would be the right thing to order for two Amkericans/(is. The Americans could only smile their gratitude.

Eventually, the waitress returned, and took the order from the man the Americans now referred to as "the colonel". Lunch turned out to be a hearty soup with potatoes, carrots and cabbage along with some tasteless bread on the side.

The soup was not bad.

By this time "the colonel" and the middle—aged lady had finished their lunches, called for their checks, and were preparing to go their separate ways.

Tony scooped up both checks and with animated gestures and smiles made it clear that he was insisting on paying for them.

The middle-aged lady gathered up her purse and belongings, gave them a lovely, grandmotherly smile, said something in Russian that sounded like goodbye, and departed. The colonel stood up. With great dignity he put on his elaborate peaked hat, nodded curtly at the two Americans, gave them a tiny, sly wink, did a military about—face and walked stiffly out of the restaurant.

For a moment, the Cold War had not been so cold.

49

IN THE FOREST

Lightning came to the forest and struck a tall, stately Virginia pine, splitting it in two and setting it afire. Mortally wounded, the giant tree fell to the forest floor.

The nearby bushes and shrubs were deeply saddened by the loss of their tall brother who had given them shade from the hot summer sun.

Their grief soon turned to terror as the flames from the fallen pine began to spread to the dry pine needles and low-lying bracken.

Father Sun, from up above, saw the danger and quickly sent Rain to extinguish the flames but some damage had been done.

Nearby plants and bushes came to the aid of the injured. Aloe Vera and Witch Hazel rubbed their soothing balms on the burns. Sister Chamomile brought calming tea. Many other plants brought their healing powers as well and soon the forest began to mend.

Even the tall pine, as it fell to its death, managed to spread some of its seeds on the forest floor and everyone knew that—with time—the forest would be whole again.

50

THE HAPPY PARADE

"Dad, where are we? This doesn't look like Wisconsin."

"I don't know for sure, Tommy."

"But what is this place?"

"I can't answer that either, son. But it looks like a nice enough place. Look at that beautiful blue sky. And the weather is fine."

"Yeah, Dad, I guess so. But I think I'd rather be home in Wisconsin"

"Look at all the other people here. Everybody is moving in the same direction. Let's follow them and see what we can find out."

Father and son followed the crowd and soon found themselves standing on the curb of what looked like a suburban street. Most of the people they had been following also took their places on the curb, as if waiting for a parade to come by. The father chatted with some of the nearby people, but nobody seemed to know where they were or what was going to happen. There was an air of excitement and expectation all about.

Presently, music, as if from a marching band, could be heard in the distance. The people in the crowd began craning their necks and looking up the street.

It was a parade! And a very happy one. The music was lively; there were clowns, jugglers. and people in gay costumes walking on stilts. The marchers were waving to the crowd, and the crowd was waving back and laughing. Everyone seemed to be having a grand old time.

The first group of marchers was dressed like old Greeks and Romans with flowing togas and sandals. Next came a group of courtly ladies and knights in shining armor carrying swords and shields. They were followed by more clowns and tumbling acrobats. Then came farm families in rough clothing and carrying old-fashioned wooden farm tools such as might be seen in a museum.

From time to time, a group of marchers would burst into joyous song accompanied by much laughter and applause from the spectators.

The father and son looked up the street. There seemed to be no end to the parade. The farmers and knights were followed by men and women wearing white collars and leg stockings. They looked like New England Pilgrims dressed for Thanksgiving.

"Dad, look, look! That man looks like George Washington. Could it really be him?

"Well, I don't know, Tommy, but you're right. He sure looks like President Washington."

Next came men dressed like pioneers in buckskin tunics and women in sunbonnets and long skirts. Mixed in with the pioneers were Indians in bright blankets and feathers. More farmers came along, then miners and factory workers and a large contingent of Civil War soldiers. Their marching band played "The Battle Hymn of the Republic" and "Nearer My God to Thee."

"Look Dad," Tommy said. "Those men are dressed like World War I soldiers."

"I see them," the father replied. "And this next group looks like the soldiers and sailors from World War II. If I didn't know better, I'd say that man looks like my old army buddy Jim O'Brien. But I know Jim is dead. He died in my arms."

"Dad, Dad, look— there's Grandpa! And Grandma is with him!"

Father and son stepped off the curb and began to march along with the older couple.

"Pop, what are you and Mom doing here?" the father asked. Where are we? And where is this parade going?"

"Well, I don't know for sure, son, but mother and I have been waiting a long time for you and Tommy to join us. We're glad you're here now. As for where this parade is going, I don't know that either, but we're having such a good time we just keep on marching along with it. Wherever it's going, it must be a pretty nice place. Why don't you and Tommy stay with us?"

They did.

And the happy-parade keeps marching along.